Meredith Webber lives on the sunny Gold Coast in Queensland, Australia, but takes regular trips west into the Outback, fossicking for gold or opal. These breaks in the beautiful and sometimes cruel red earth country provide her with an escape from the writing desk and a chance for her mind to roam free—not to mention getting some much needed exercise. They also supply the kernels of so many stories it's hard for her to stop writing!

A MIRACLE FOR THE BABY DOCTOR

BY
MEREDITH WEBBER

MILLS & BOON

First published in Great Britain 2017
by Mills & Boon, an imprint of HarperCollins*Publishers*
1 London Bridge Street, London, SE1 9GF

Large Print edition 2018

© 2017 Meredith Webber

ISBN: 978-0-263-07255-6

MIX
Paper from
responsible sources
FSC® C007454

This book is produced from independently certified
FSC™ paper to ensure responsible forest management. For
more information visit www.harpercollins.co.uk/green.

Printed and bound in Great Britain
by CPI Group (UK) Ltd, Croydon, CR0 4YY

34756353

PROLOGUE

FRANCESCA LOUISE HAWTHORNE put down the phone with a sigh.

A deep sigh!

Why had she stayed in Sydney?

Why hadn't she fled to the far ends of the earth after the divorce?

Sheer stubborn pride, probably!

She shrugged her shoulders and sighed again. 'Trouble?'

She turned at the sound of her boss's voice and smiled at the man who was part of the reason she *hadn't* fled. Dr Andrew Flint was one of the foremost IVF specialists in Australia—the best in Sydney as far as Fran was concerned—and his, admittedly early, work into IVM could revolutionise the way couples who had difficulty conceiving could have babies.

Could bring hope…

And she knew a lot about hope…

Andy had been the first specialist in Australia to work on in vitro maturation, where immature eggs were taken from women and grown to maturity in an incubator, and this work had excited Fran so much she hadn't considered leaving.

'Andy?' she said, when he'd been standing just inside the door of her office for a few moments.

This prompt was obviously not enough so she added, 'You wanted something?'

He smiled and shook his head.

'I did, but now I'm realising just how much I'll miss you if you say yes to what I've come to ask.'

Fran shook her head. Used as she was to deciphering her rather absent-minded boss's pronouncements, this one had her stumped.

'Which was?' she tried.

He was still smiling as he came closer to her.

'I've been asked to lend you to someone. Have you ever run across Steve Ransome? He runs an IVF clinic in the Alexandria area. He offers couples on limited incomes from some of the inner-city areas a reduced rate but his clinic has a high success rate so he has plenty of regular fee-paying clients.'

Fran shook her head.

'Doesn't ring a bell,' she said, refusing to think about high success rates and concentrating instead on where on earth this conversation might be going.

And why had he mentioned missing her?

At least trying to make sense out of Andy's rambling was distracting her from the mother's phone call—from the image of a smugly pregnant Clarissa that had lodged in her head...

'Well, no matter, he's a good bloke, and he's asked me to lend you to him.'

'Lend me to him?'

This was bizarre, even for Andy!

'For his clinic in Vanuatu.'

Andy made this pronouncement as if it cleared up the whole conversation, and beamed at her as if he'd managed something wonderful.

Fran rose to her feet and walked around her desk, pulling up a chair and turning to her boss.

'Please sit, Andy, then tell me this story from the beginning. I gather this doctor contacted you. Let's start there.'

Looking mildly put out, Andy sat.

'But I told you,' he protested. 'Vanuatu! Only for a few weeks—four, I think Steve said. I thought it would be great for you—tropical island, balmy breezes, getting out of Sydney when the weather's so lousy. It's work, of course, and he particularly asked if I had someone on staff who'd done some IVM work. I thought of you straight off. You've been looking a little peaky lately. The change will do you good. Hard to manage here without you, of course, but you've got all the staff trained so well, I'm sure they'll cope.'

Sufficiently intrigued to swallow yet another sigh, Fran pieced the random bits of information together.

'This man has a clinic in Vanuatu?'

Andy smiled again, practically applauding her grip on the situation.

'It's a giving-back thing, you see, or maybe

paying forward—that's what he might have said,' he said, and although Fran didn't see or follow the paying forward part, she pressed on.

'And he needs an embryologist for four weeks?'

'I think it was four, or maybe six,' Andy said, his forehead crumpling as he tried to remember. Then he obviously gave up on that bit of irrelevant information and added, 'I said I was pretty sure you'd go. Friend in need—doing good work—that kind of thing. Right up your alley, I thought, and a lovely holiday thrown in.'

Realising she wasn't going to get much more from her boss, Fran changed tack.

'Perhaps I should speak to him, find out exactly what the job entails.'

Andy shook his head.

'Afraid not,' he said. 'He left yesterday. Asked me last week but I forgot and he phoned from the airport. Gave me the name of his practice manager and said she'd sort you out with flights and stuff. I've got the number here.'

Andy fished in his pocket, producing several screwed-up scraps of paper, uncrumpling them and glancing at each for a moment before stuffing them back into their hiding place.

'Ah, here we go! Name's Helen and the phone number's there.'

He handed the scrap of paper to Fran, who surveyed it dubiously. It certainly said Helen and there *was* a phone number but…

'I think he wants you soon—like yesterday,' Andy added, standing up and heading for the door. 'You'll still get your pay from here, of course, and he said something about having accommodation for you. Do keep in touch.'

On which note he disappeared out the door.

Having worked with Andy since graduating ten years earlier, Fran knew that was all she'd get out of him. In fact, if she asked him anything about it later in the day, he would probably stare blankly at her, the entire conversation lost in whatever was currently holding his attention.

So Fran leaned back in her chair and wondered about serendipity.

Ten minutes earlier she'd been pondering her stupidity in letting pride keep her in Sydney after her divorce from Nigel and his subsequent marriage to Clarissa.

Well, pride, and her attachment to Andy and his work!

Now here was an invitation to escape—if only for four weeks—plumped right into her lap in the most unlikely manner.

Piecing together what little she'd gleaned from Andy, she assumed this man he'd spoken of—Steve Ransome—was running some kind of IVF programme on the island of Vanuatu and needed a embryologist—in particular one with experience in the very new field of IVM.

She knew of Vanuatu, of course. An island nation in the South Pacific, originally under French rule, if she remembered rightly.

Sun, sand, crystal-clear water, palm-tree fronds waving languidly over brilliantly coloured flowers…

She looked at the rain lashing against her window and shivered because September, which should be bringing a little warmth, and a promise of spring, had so far provided nothing but rain and more rain, with temperatures more like winter.

And Clarissa was pregnant...

Her ex-husband's wife, Clarissa.

Her ex-husband, who'd hated every visit to the IVF clinic when Fran had been trying to get pregnant, who'd found the whole idea of IVF somehow humiliating—a slight on his manhood—and who now had a naturally pregnant wife...

And as Fran's mother's best friend, Joan, was Nigel's mother, there'd no doubt be regular progress reports on the pregnancy of the wonderfully fertile Clarissa.

Doubt stabbed at her, making Fran wonder if the whole thing subtly underlined her mother's disappointment in Fran's failure to produce a child. Fran shook her head again.

No, her mother had been upset over the divorce, but more because of the two families' friendship.

But the friendship had survived between her mother and Joan and although her mother was nearly always travelling these days, they were obviously still in close contact. Blame mobile phones and the internet!

Which meant Fran would doubtless get updates on the pregnancy at regular intervals, each one probing all the still sore spots in Fran's heart and mind.

Getting away, if only for a month, was exactly what she needed.

Although...

She looked around the lab, seeing her workmates busy at their jobs.

After all the treatment she'd had, plus three unsuccessful IVF cycles, people had been surprised that she'd come back to work.

To work that was such an integral part of IVF programmes.

But here, in the big lab that dealt with so many specimens and eggs and tiny embryos to care for, she didn't ever know which couple had success, and who had failed. She was shut off from their success or their pain.

And her own remembered pain...

Fran smoothed out the piece of paper, checked the number and phoned a stranger called Helen.

CHAPTER ONE

STEVE PARKED THE battered four-wheel drive in the short-stay area of the car park and hurried towards the arrivals hall.

When he realised he hadn't a clue what the woman he was to meet looked like, he hurried back to the car, tore the top off a carton and hurriedly scrawled 'Dr Hawthorne' on it.

Okay, so the name on a card made him look like a limo driver, except that in flip-flops, shorts and a vivid print shirt he didn't even come close to their tailored elegance.

And the limo drivers, he noticed, now he was back in the crowd outside the customs area, were holding professionally printed signs.

He should have done better. After all, this woman was doing him a huge favour, coming out here on a moment's notice to cover for his usual embryologist.

He could at least have worn a quieter shirt.

It was the pelican's fault!

He'd been heading for the shower when two young boys had appeared with an injured pelican—hauling it behind them in a homemade go-cart. The bird had appeared to have an injured wing but its docility had made Steve suspect it had other injuries as well.

He'd explained to the boys that they needed a vet, then realised they could hardly drag it all the way to the north of the island where the vet had his practice. Packing all three of them—and the cart—into his car and driving them out there had seemed the only solution, which had left him too late to shower and change.

So now he was late, and probably smelling of fish.

It couldn't be helped. He was sure the woman would understand…

Passengers began to emerge, and he studied each one. The holidaymakers were obvious, already in party mode, smiling and laughing as they came through the doors, looking around eagerly for their first glimpse of the tropical paradise. Returning locals he could also pick out quite easily. Men in business suits or harassed mothers herding troops of children.

Then came a tall woman, light brown hair slicked back into some kind of neat arrangement at the back of her head, loose slacks and a blue shirt, a hard-case silver suitcase wheeling along behind her.

Elegant. Sophisticated.

Not Dr Hawthorne, he decided, as the embryologists he knew were more the absent-minded professor type, usually clad in distressed jeans and band name T-shirts beneath their lab coats.

The elegant woman paused, scanning the names held up in the crowd, passed by his and started towards someone else.

It was stupid to feel disappointed, there were plenty more passengers to come. Apart from which, she'd be a work colleague—work being the operative word.

'Dr Ransome?'

He turned, and there was the woman, strange green eyes studying him quite intensely.

Green?

He checked—maybe blue, not green, or blue-green, hard to tell.

'You *are* Dr Ransome?' she said with an edge of impatience. 'Helen told me you would meet me.'

'Sorry, yes,' Steve said, and held out his hand, realising too late that it was still holding his makeshift sign.

'Oops,' he said, tucking the sign under his arm.

He reached out to take the handle of her suitcase.

'The car's out this way,' he said, heading for the door. 'It was so good of you to come—so good of Andy to spare you. My usual embryologist had a skiing accident in New Zealand last month and is still in traction.'

Was he talking too much?

He usually did when he was rattled, and the

cool, sophisticated woman walking beside him had rattled every bone in his body.

But why, for heaven's sake? It wasn't that there weren't—or hadn't been—other such women in his life.

He slid a sidelong glance towards her.

Composed, that's what she was, which put him at a disadvantage as, right now, he was…well, badly dressed and almost certainly in need of a shower. The boys had been trying to feed the bird small fish.

'Sorry about the rough sign, not to mention the clothes. There was this pelican, you see…'

She obviously didn't see, probably wasn't even listening.

He changed tack.

'Do you know Vanuatu? It's a great place—not only the islands themselves but the people. Originally settled by the French, so many people still speak that language, although they speak English as well—tourism has made sure of that.'

He reached the battered vehicle and immediately wished it was more impressive—a limo perhaps.

Because she looked like a woman who'd drive in limos rather than battered four-wheel drives?

But some demon of uncertainty had set up home in his mind, and he heard himself apologising.

'Sorry it's not a limo, but the budget is always tight and I'd rather spend money on the clinic.'

'Sounds reasonable to me,' she said coolly.

He lifted the silver case into the rear, and came around to open the door for her, but she was already climbing in. Elegantly.

He held the door while she settled herself, then held out his hand.

'I'm sorry, I don't even know what to call you. It's been a strange morning.'

She offered a cool smile but did take his hand in a firm clasp.

'Francesca,' she said. 'But just call me Fran.'

He forcibly withdrew his hand, which had wanted to linger in hers, and closed the door.

But not before noticing that her hair was coming just slightly loose from its restraints, a golden-brown strand curling around to touch her chin.

The sun would streak it paler still. And suddenly he pictured this woman on one of the island's deserted beaches, a sarong wrapped around her bikini, sun streaks in the hair blowing back from her face as she walked beside him.

His body stirred and he shook his head at the fantasy. For a start she was a colleague, and just looking at her he could see she was hardly the 'strolling on the beach in a sarong' type, not that that stopped the stirring.

'Have you been to the islands before?' he asked, as he settled behind the wheel, coaxed a muted grumble from the engine, and drove towards the exit gates.

'No, although I know many Australians holiday here.'

'I hope you'll like it. The climate's great, although it can get a trifle hot at times, and the people are wonderful.'

She turned towards him, the blue-green eyes

taking in his bright shirt and, no doubt, the stubble on his unshaven chin.

The pelican again…

'Did you holiday here? Is that why you've come back here to work?'

He smiled, remembering his co-workers' disbelief when he'd told them of his plans to start the clinic.

'No, but we had a couple—Vanuatuans—who came to my clinic in Sydney. They were so desperate to have a child they had sold everything they had, including the fishing boat that was their livelihood, to fund their trip.'

The words pierced the armour Fran had built around her heart and she felt again the pain of not conceiving. Of not having the child she'd so wanted.

You're over this, she reminded herself, and concentrated on Steve's explanation.

'But to sell their boat—their livelihood?'

He turned more fully to her now, and the compassion she read in his face warmed her to the man with whom she would work—a scruffy, unshaven, slightly smelly, yet still a darkly attractive man.

Attractive?

What was she thinking?

But he was speaking, explaining.

'Why not sell the boat if they had no child to inherit it?' he said softly, and she felt the barb go deeper into her heart.

She nodded, thinking of the couple.

'Few people consider the side-effects of infertility,' she said softly, remembering. 'The loss of self-esteem, the feelings of pointlessness, the loss of libido that failure can cause, which must be devastating for any man, but would, I imagine, be even worse for people of proud warrior races like the islanders.'

He glanced her way, questions in his eyes, and she realised she'd spoken too passionately—come too close to giving herself away.

Talk work—that was the answer.

'So you came here? But not permanently? How does that work?'

He smiled.

'You'll see, but for now you should be looking about you, not talking work. This is Vila, capital of the island nation. You can still see a lot of the old buildings that have survived from the days the French ran the country.'

Fran looked around obediently and was soon charmed by the riot of colour in the gardens around all the buildings, from small huts to old colonial buildings, no longer white but grey with age, some in a state of disrepair, but all boasting trailing bougainvillea in rich red or purple, and white lilies running riot in unkempt garden beds. Ferns and big-leafed plants provided lush greenery, so altogether Fran's immediate impression was one of colour.

They drove up a hill, the buildings becoming smaller and more suburban, and right at the top sat what could only be a mansion with another large building further along the ridge.

They turned that way and an ambulance streaking towards it told her it was the hospital.

'Is the clinic at the hospital?' she asked.

'Not quite—but we're around the back here. A

kind of adjunct to it,' her chauffeur told her. 'Our building used to be nurses' quarters but the hospital doesn't have live-in nurses any more.'

He pulled up in a driveway beside an enormous red bougainvillea that had wound its way up a tall tree.

Colour everywhere!

And warmth, she realised as she stepped out of the vehicle.

A warmth that wrapped, blanket-like, around her.

They had stopped beside a run-down building that seemed to ramble down the hill behind the hospital. It had cracks in the once white walls, and dark, damp-looking patches where plaster had fallen off. Vines seemed to be growing out of the top of it, and the overall impression was of desertion and decay.

A tall local man came out to greet the car, holding out his hand to Fran.

'I am Akila. I am the caretaker here and will also take care of you,' he said, pride deepening an already deep voice. 'We are very pleased to have you come and work with us.'

He waved his hand towards the building.

'Outside this must look bad to you, but wait until you see inside,' Akila told her, obviously aware of strangers' first impressions.

And he was right.

The foyer was painted bright yellow, making it seem as if the sunshine from outside had penetrated the gloomy walls. A huge urn of flowers—long stems of something sweet-scented and vividly red—stood against the far wall, grabbing Fran's attention the moment she came through the door.

A cheerful young woman appeared in a brightly flowered long flowing dress Fran recognised as a muumuu. Zoe hugged Fran as Steve introduced her.

'This is where we live when we're here. Zoe will show you our quarters. Both she and Akila live locally and work at the hospital, but come down to help out when we are working on the island,' Steve said. 'Zoe keeps the place tidy for us and makes sure there is always food in the cupboards and refrigerator so we don't starve to death, while Akila is on call for any emergencies—of which we get plenty—power outages, et cetera. But don't worry we have generators which kick in to keep your incubator warm.'

Fran felt a niggle of apprehension, and for a moment longed to be back in her nice, safe, *big*, anonymous lab. These people were all too friendly. They were a team, but clearly friends as well. Why hadn't she considered that it would be a small and intimate staff in this island clinic?

Friendly!

A queasy feeling in her stomach reminded her just how long it had been since she'd done friendly! At first, the pain of the IVF failures had made her curl into herself, erecting a cool polite barrier that outsiders saw.

Then the divorce and the humiliating knowledge that Nigel and Clarissa had been involved for months had made her draw away from the few friends she hadn't shut out earlier. The only good thing that had come out of the whole mess was a better understanding of her mother, who had also built a protective shell around herself when *her* husband had departed. At last she now understood her mother's detached behaviour during her childhood years.

Hurt prevention…

Fran had drifted across the hall to touch the leaves and flowers in the big display while these thoughts tumbled through her head.

'I will show you your room,' Zoe said, bringing Fran abruptly back to the present.

'And I've got to check on something but I'll be over later and will take you through the whole facility then,' Steve added.

Fran felt a new wave of…not panic perhaps but definite uncertainty. Did she really need to see the whole facility? Of course she wanted to see the laboratory—it was where she would be working—and seeing how the place was set up would be interesting, but…

Something about the warm friendliness of the people was beginning to unsettle her—the realisation that they were all one big happy family, with Steve at the centre of it. It was threatening to cause cracks in barriers she had carefully erected between herself and others.

And all because they were *welcoming* her, were *friendly*? She could hardly resent that...

It had to be the heat, she decided, following Zoe across a courtyard filled with rioting plants, most with broad leaves and drooping fronds of flowers, and the same sweet, indefinable perfume.

'Ginger,' Zoe explained when Fran asked, and she looked more closely at the plants, not exactly surprised but trying to relate the small, bulbous roots she bought at the greengrocer to these exuberant, leafy plants.

The living quarters were adequate, freshly painted and clean, two bedrooms, a shared bathroom—she could live with that—and a combined living, dining, kitchen area.

'Steve, he barbecues,' Zoe told her, leading Fran out the back door onto a beautiful, shaded deck area, with a barbecue bigger and more complex than the kitchen back at her flat. 'He brought the barbecue here but it is for everyone who stays.

Patients bring fish and chicken and he says they are best on barbecue.'

Fran smiled. It was obvious the giant barbecue was the subject of much conversation among the staff at the clinic.

Zoe then indicated which bedroom would be hers and left her to unpack. It was a spacious room, with two beds—king singles or small doubles, she couldn't tell—two wooden dressers with drawers, and a built-in cupboard. A vase filled with wide leaves and bright flowers stood on one of the dressers, welcoming her.

Uncertain of what lay ahead, Fran opted not to shower but simply to freshen up. She unclipped her hair, then made her way to the bathroom. She'd washed her face and was brushing out her hair when Steve arrived, calling hello from the front door.

She came out of her room, hairbrush still in her hand, anxious to tell him she'd only be a moment.

Steve stood in the doorway. Okay, so he'd assumed she'd be a very attractive woman with her hair waving softly around her face, but *this* attractive? She was smiling, saying something, but all he could do was stand and gawp.

Fortunately for his peace of mind she disappeared back into her room, returning seconds later with her hair neatly restrained, though this time more casually in a low ponytail at the base of her skull, one tail of the scarf that held it dangling forward over her white shirt, drawing his attention to—

No, his attention wasn't going there.

'I'll show you our set-up,' he said, aware his voice sounded rough. And why wouldn't it because his mouth, for surely the first time in his life, had gone dry.

But his pride in the little clinic diverted his mind away from Fran as a very attractive woman—or almost diverted it—while he showed her around the rooms.

'It's very well set out, and far more complex than I'd imagined. You spoke about the couple who came to you in Sydney for IVF, and wanting to have something here, but this is impressive—

it's got everything you need, just on a smaller scale.'

'I wanted to set up a place where couples can come and have their infertility investigated right from the start,' he explained. 'I can't help feeling people are sometimes prey to exploitation. As you know, the most common cause of women not ovulating is PCO, and polycystic ovary syndrome can be treated with drugs. I believe, before IVF is even mentioned, ethical specialists must determine the underlying cause of the problem, and if possible treat it.'

Fran gave a little shake of her head. These were thoughts she'd had herself. Not that any of the specialists she'd seen had been unethical, but it had often seemed to her that they rushed towards IVF as an answer without considering alternatives.

'I imagine drugs like clomiphene are a case in point,' she said, seeing the way his mind worked. 'With very little in the way of side-effects they can encourage the production of follicle-stimulating hormone, so the ovaries are better able to

produce follicles. That in itself can lead to a previously infertile couple conceiving.'

'Or, unfortunately, it could sometimes lead
to cysts in the ovaries, which means the patient
needs to be checked regularly. That's why we em-
ploy a full-time O and G specialist who works
at the hospital as well as here at the clinic. We
want to be able to take a patient right through any
treatment available, even Fallopian tube repairs,
before resorting to IVF.'

'So you need a specialist on the ground, so
to speak?' Fran said, following the conversation
with increasing interest.

'Exactly! He does regular obstetric and gynae
work at the hospital but he's also available for all
the preliminary IVF checks and organises the
counselling all couples need, as well as supervising the weeks of injections for any woman who
will be using IVF.'

'Wow!' Fran muttered, unable to believe so
much was happening from this small, run-down-
looking building.

She looked again at the scruffily dressed man, and shook her head.

'Did you achieve all of this on your own?' she asked, and he smiled at her.

The smile surprised her. She'd seen versions of it before and thought it a nice smile, but this one set his whole face alight, shining in his dark eyes and wrinkling his cheeks with the width of his grin.

'Not quite,' he admitted. 'The partners back at my clinic in Sydney have given a lot in that they cover for me two or three times a year when I'm over here, and various patients I've had have talked to me about what they'd like in a clinic.'

She nodded, knowing exactly what she'd have liked in the places she'd seen so much of, but Steve was still talking.

'Then there are the people here. They are laid-back, casual and very family-oriented so something like an inability to have a child can cause them tremendous pain. I knew I had to set things up to make it as relaxed as possible for them. After all, they are the prime concern.'

'And you fund it all yourself?'

The question was out before she realised how rude it was.

Not that it appeared to bother him—he just ignored it.

'And here's the laboratory, such as it is,' Steve announced,

He'd left it until last, hoping she'd want to stay on and have a look around, check out where things were kept and see from the case notes, both written and on the computer, how things were done. Then he could go back to their quarters and, no, he refused to consider the cliché of a cold shower, but he could get away from her for a while and regroup.

Work out why this unlikely attraction was happening.

Attraction should be something that grew as you got to know someone—grew out of liking and respect...

Forget attraction, getting rid of the fish smell and doing something about the stubble on his chin were far more important issues right now.

Oh, *and* catching up with Alex to find out whether their new equipment had arrived...

But still he looked at Fran, bent over the boxes of coloured tags she'd pulled from one of the cupboards. She poked around in the contents for a while, then glanced up at him and smiled.

So much for his thoughts on attraction...

'You'll probably laugh at me,' she was saying, 'but I brought a whole heap of these things with me in my luggage, thinking maybe you wouldn't have the ones I've always used, but someone whose mind runs along the same lines as mine does has set up a basic identification system.'

'That someone was me.'

She looked surprised, and, probably because he was already off balance with the attraction business, he spoke more sharply than he need have.

'Lab staff aren't the only ones afraid of making a mistake, of giving a woman someone else's embryo. It's always in the back of my mind, even in the clinic back home where everything is computerised to the nth degree and ID is made with bar codes.'

Now she was taken aback, frowning at him.

'Of course you must worry, it's everyone's biggest concern, but usually it's left to the lab staff to make sure mistakes don't happen.' She grinned at him, defusing his mild annoyance but aggravating the attraction. 'It's certainly the lab staff who get blamed when things go wrong.'

She lifted a red wristband, a red marking pen, a roll of red plastic tape and a card of small red spots.

'How many patients are you expecting? I know you said earlier, but I can't recall the number,' she said. 'I'll make up packs of what we need for each of them—that way I won't be fishing in boxes later and will be less likely to make a mistake.'

She was here to work and she was making that abundantly clear, which was good as he could forget all the weirdness he'd been experiencing and get on with *his* job.

'Five, or maybe six,' he told her. 'I've just heard that there's one couple we're not sure about. Apparently it took longer than expected to shut down her ovaries and then to begin the stimulation so she may not be ovulating yet.'

'But surely she would be before we leave?' Francesca asked, the slight frown he was beginning to recognise as one of concern puckering her forehead.

'Yes, and although I do have other volunteers come out here to work, we like to have the same team on hand for the whole cycle of taking the eggs through to implantation, then confirmation of pregnancy.'

'Or confirmation that it didn't work that time,' Fran said, remembering her three thwarted attempts.

'That too,' Steve said, his voice sombre. 'It's the main reason I like the team to stay until we know, one way or another. At least then we can talk to the couple about what they would like to do next. Whether they want to try again later— explain the options, talk it all through with them.'

He'd really thought about it, Fran thought, studying the man who seemed to understand just how devastating a failed IVF treatment could be.

But couldn't they still work with the sixth couple? Hadn't Andy said...?

'But rather than have them miss out, couldn't we stay a little longer?' she asked. 'I'm sure Andy said that it could be longer—six weeks he might have mentioned. Wouldn't that give us time?'

Fran realised she was probably pushing too hard—especially as a newcomer. But it seemed inconceivable to her that a woman would get this far into treatment then be told they couldn't go ahead until Steve could return or someone else could come over.

Steve shook his head, but it wasn't the head-shake that bothered her, it was the look on his face—discouragement?

'And if six weeks isn't long enough?' he said quietly.

'Then we'd just have to stay on,' Fran declared. 'I know you must feel guilty about leaving your own practice longer than necessary, but a few days? Surely we can't just ignore this couple as if they're nothing more than names on a list.'

She waited for a reply, but all Steve did was look at her, studying her as if she was a stranger.

Had she let emotion seep into her words? She knew, better than anyone, that she had to separate her emotion from her work—that she had to be one hundred per cent focussed on whatever job she was doing—no room for emotion at all. But hadn't her argument been rational?

'Let's wait and see,' he finally replied, but he was still watching her warily.

Assessing her in some way...

Wondering if he'd made a serious mistake in asking for her...

He turned and walked away, leaving her with all the red markers in her hands, no doubt remembering she'd said she wanted to sort the separate colours into packs. Well, she did intend to do that. Keeping track of everything in the laboratory was of prime importance, and as far as she was concerned, the laboratory's responsibility stretched across every sample taken. So she settled on a stool, marking syringes, specimen jars, test tubes, specimen dishes—everything—

with coloured stickers or tape or even paint for things that wouldn't hold the coloured tape.

But her fingers stilled, and she looked towards the door through which Steve Ransome had disappeared.

Was it because he thought as she did about fertility treatments, or because he obviously cared so much about his patients that she found him attractive?

She considered the word. Certainly he was tall and well built, with dark hair, and eyes set deep beneath thick black brows. Nice enough nose, good chin...

But carelessly dressed, unshaven—scruffy!

Scruffily attractive?

Work, she reminded herself.

Five couples, five colours—no, she'd do six. Mr and Mrs Number Six were going to get just as good treatment as the others. Red, green, blue, purple, yellow and brown—she never used black as somewhere along the chain someone might use a black pen to write a note on a sample and confuse things. From this point on she usually thought of the couples in colours—Mr and Mrs Yellow's egg might be dividing beautifully, Mr Green's sperm was very healthy.

It made sense, especially in a foreign country where the names might be difficult to pronounce, and it kept things clear in her mind. A psychologist would tell her she did it to prevent herself bonding too closely with the couples and that was probably true as well, but her main function was to run the lab efficiently so every couple had the best chance of success. She packaged up what would be needed for each coloured couple, turning her mind now to all the questions she hadn't asked Steve.

Normal questions, like did they add a little serum from the mother's blood to the media in which they'd place the egg, and was serum extracted from the blood on site or at the hospital? It was a job she could do and she had a feeling adaptability was an essential attribute when working here, but was this lab purely for the fertilisation and maturation process or was it multi-purpose?

She finished her packages, two for each colour, one for use by the nurses and doctor interacting with the couples, and one for lab use, and went in search of Steve, wandering around the little clinic first, checking the procedure room, the ultrasound machine Steve would use to measure the size of the women's follicles to see if an egg was ready for collection, then use again to guide him when collecting them.

He'd lamented not having a laparoscope and perhaps when she returned home she could find an organisation willing to donate one.

'Were you looking for me?'

He was so close behind her that when she spun around she all but fell against him, needing to put her hand on his chest to steady herself.

Something sparked in Steve's eyes but she was too concerned with her own reactions to be thinking of his. The long-dormant embers of desire that an earlier smile had brought back to life flared yet again.

With nothing more than an accidental touch?

He mustn't guess!

That was her first thought.

So cover up!

That was her second.

Although it was far too late. They'd stood, her hand against his chest, for far too long, the tension she could feel in her body matched by what she felt in his—something arcing through the air between them—pulsing, electric.

She stepped back, sure she must be losing her mind that such fantasy could flash through it.

Talk work!

'I was thinking I could probably find an organisation or service club back home that could donate a laparoscope,' she said, backing off as far as the doorjamb would allow.

'It would come in handy, especially as a diagnostic tool,' he said, ice cool for all she'd seen something flicker in his eyes, and felt the tension—sure she'd felt an accelerated pulse. 'But since I started coming here, I've become adept at removing eggs with the ultrasound to guide me.'

'Imagine going back to the days when women needed an operation to remove them, sometimes in the middle of the night, because ovulation wasn't timed as well as it is today.'

This was good, carrying on a normal conversation with him for all the sudden heat and awareness flaring inside her.

'There are some funny stories of those days,' he said, smiling at her, although he seemed slightly surprised that she knew the history of IVF.

But, then, he didn't know *her* history.

He didn't know anything about her, which made her feel just a little sad as she walked with him across the courtyard towards their quarters.

'So, if you've seen enough, how about I take you for a quick drive around the town and we grab something to eat down on the foreshore? There's a great French restaurant on the front that most of the visiting staff use as a home away from home.'

'But Zoe said that monster barbecue is yours— that you cook?'

He grinned at her, alerting all the bits she'd just damped down.

'You make it sound somehow shameful,' he

protested. 'I enjoy cooking—well, barbecuing—and patients bring us food so I feel obliged to cook it. Some of them have so little, yet they give whatever they can. But tonight there's no free gift so we might as well eat out.'

He hesitated for a moment, then said, 'You probably want to shower and change before we go. We'll leave in an hour? Is that okay with you?'

'I won't need an hour to shower and change,' she said. 'Embryologists still get called out at night from time to time, so I've retained my get up and go skills.'

He smiled again, something she was beginning to wish he wouldn't do because being attracted to a man she'd only just met was ridiculous. Just as ridiculous as reacting to something as simple as a smile.

'Ah, but in our case, remember, we share the bathroom, and after a morning wrestling with a pelican I, too, need to use it.'

'A pelican?'

'I'll tell you later,' he said, and for some obscure reason it sounded like a special promise.

'So the shower? You'll use it first?' he prompted, before adding with a teasing grin, 'Unless, of course, we shower together.'

She didn't blush—she hadn't, even when she was young—but she knew if she was a blushing type she'd have been ruby red. Not that she could let him guess *that* reaction.

'And wouldn't the other staff view that as unprofessional behaviour?' she asked, hoping she sounded far cooler than she felt.

'Maybe they wouldn't know,' he replied, the teasing note lingering in his voice. 'They don't live in, you know.'

He wasn't serious, she was one hundred per cent sure of that, yet there'd been an undertone in his voice that unsettled her even more than she was already unsettled.

An undertone she didn't want to think about.

Except the conversation did suggest that he *had* felt whatever it was that had arced between them…

'I just want to check something back at the lab,' she said, turning on the spot and hurrying away, calling over her shoulder, 'so you can have first shower.'

She was being ridiculous.

As if he'd be interested in her.

It was his way. Teasing and maybe a bit flirtatious—laid-back like the islanders—he was that kind of man.

Could she flirt back?

The idea excited her but deep down she knew she couldn't play that game. She'd never been able to flirt.

Oh, for Pete's sake, what was she doing, standing in this makeshift lab having a mental conversation with herself about flirting!

CHAPTER TWO

SHE STALKED BACK to the little apartment and shut herself in the bedroom where she stared at her 'casual' clothes and realised just how different the concept of 'casual' was here in the islands. Thinking of photographs she'd seen of Pacific islands, she'd thrown in one long, silky shift, not as voluminous as the muumuus all the women seemed to wear, but at least it would look more relaxed than slacks. It was pretty, too, a mix of blue and green in colour, a gift from a friend who'd claimed she'd bought it for herself before she realised the colours didn't suit her.

It was still unworn because it was then that Fran had found out about Nigel and Clarissa—such a cliché that had been! Coming home from work early because she wasn't feeling well! Desperately hoping it was a sign that she was pregnant—the test kit in her handbag—and Clarissa in her bed!

To make it a thousand times worse, the test strip had been, like all the others, negative...

So the lovely new shift had been inevitably tied to that devastating day and had been consigned to the back of her wardrobe.

At least now she could laugh about it—almost!

'Bathroom's free!'

Damnation! Even the man's voice was unnerving her. But as long as he didn't realise the effect he was having on her, it wouldn't matter, would it?

She had a shower and pulled on the dress, brushed her hair and turned to the mirror so she could twist it into a neat knot on the top of her head, but upswept hair didn't go with the neckline of the dress and she let her hair fall so it brushed her shoulders and hung softly about her face.

Yes, it went with the dress this way, but was the woman in the mirror really her? And if not, was she being someone else because she was going out to dinner with an attractive man?

An attractive *stranger*, she reminded herself.

The questions racing through her mind left her as nervous and uncertain as a teenager on her first date, and it was *that* thought which brought a return to sanity.

It was *not* a date, she was *not* a teenager. Steve was a colleague, nothing more. She swept the brush through her hair again, hauling it back, but the restraining rubber band she'd been going to use to hold it while she twisted it into a knot had slipped from her fingers and as she bent forward, searching the floor for it, she heard a knock on the far bathroom door and heard Steve's voice.

'Hour's up,' he said, and although she was fairly certain he was teasing and not desperate to get going, she opened the door, her hair still held up in her hands.

'Lost the band,' she explained, 'but I've more in my luggage. Won't be a minute.'

'Leave your hair down—you're in the islands,' he said. 'The expression "hang loose" belongs in

Hawaii rather than Vanuatu, but it's just as pertinent here. Everything's fluid—time in particular—and once you get used to the fact that a ten o'clock appointment might arrive at eleven-thirty you'll be surprised how relaxed you become.'

The idea of an appointment being more than an hour late horrified her, but maybe she *could* get used to it.

Maybe.

She'd think about that later. In the meantime…

'And this has what to do with my hair?'

'Let it hang loose,' he suggested, producing the gentle smile that melted her bones. 'Let it hang loose and we'll find a flower to put behind your ear.'

There was a longish pause, during which she actually let go of her hair, running her fingers through it so it fell without tangles, wanting to tell him she wasn't a flower behind the ear kind of person, but before she could say anything he spoke again.

'Of course it will be up to you to decide which ear,' he said, leaving Fran so bemused she fled to her bedroom, muttering something about fetching her handbag while her mind searched for the source of the little ping it had given when he'd spoken of flowers and ears.

It *did* mean something, but in her befuddled state she had no idea what. She'd just have to hope they didn't find a flower so she wouldn't have to make a fool of herself doing the wrong thing.

She was stunning.

Steve watched her beat a hasty retreat into her bedroom, the long, silky dress clinging to the curves of her body, her hair, darkish but shot with light, bouncing on her shoulders.

This was the second time he'd seen her in the bathroom doorway with a brush in her hand, yet this time…

Maybe it was the dress. This time, with her arms raised to hold her hair, she'd reminded him of a painting he'd once seen, or a statue, something of spectacular beauty that had stuck in his mind, yet she seemed totally unaware of her allure.

Which made her all the more attractive...

There had to be at least a dozen reasons why he shouldn't get involved with this woman. At the top of the list was the probability that she wasn't interested in him, then the fact that they worked together, and he wasn't in the market for a serious relationship just yet, and he was fairly certain she was a serious relationship kind of person.

Although...

Experience told him that it was rare to be drawn to a woman who wasn't interested in him—attraction as strong as he was feeling was almost always mutual and although Francesca Hawthorne had given no hint of interest in him, he could put that down to the fact that women were more reluctant to reveal how they felt, as if being physically attracted to a man was somehow shameful.

Particularly, he guessed, women like Francesca.

Or was he kidding himself?

There was only one way to find out. He headed into the garden in search of a flower...

'Which ear?' he asked when he returned, brandishing the bright red hibiscus in front of Francesca.

'What do you mean, which ear?' she demanded, causing him to wonder if she would be bossy in bed?

The thought was so irrelevant—so irrational—he shocked even himself, yet he couldn't help a surge of anticipation as well.

'Availability,' he explained, coming closer to her, breathing in the scent of woman beneath a light, flowery fragrance that might be nothing more than hair shampoo. 'It's an age-old custom—right ear for available women, left ear if you're taken. Left because it's closer to the heart, and in truth it's probably a tourist legend, not a local custom at all.'

He was too close. Fran's nerves were skirmishing with her brain, urging her to move closer, while her brain yelled for restraint.

Restraint!

It was practically a byword in her life, preached by her mother, confirmed by her husband, restraint in everything.

Not that her ex-husband had shown any restraint when it came to Clarissa…

Did that explain this sudden urge to fling it all away? To move out of the confining bounds of the life she'd always led? To forget the stupid guilt she'd felt when her father had left her and her mother, and the restraint she'd imposed on herself since that day.

Don't rock the boat had become her motto.

Foolishly?

'Definitely not taken,' she muttered, disturbed as much by the memories and the fight within her as the closeness of the attractive man.

'Good,' he said quietly as he slid the flower's delicate stem behind her right ear, letting his fingers brush against her jaw as he withdrew his hand, his eyes holding hers, sending messages she didn't want to understand.

Or didn't want to acknowledge?

'Now, should we drive or walk? It's up to you. The walk down is beautiful because you look out over the town and the sea, but coming back up the hill isn't fun if you're tired after your flight.'

Fran took his words as a challenge. Tired after her flight indeed!

'I hope I'm not so feeble I can't manage a flight *and* a walk up a hill all in one day,' she retorted, trying in vain to remember just how high the hill they'd driven up earlier might be.

Ha! So she's got some spirit, this sophisticated beauty, Steve thought, though all he said was, 'That's great.'

They set off, up past the hospital, along the ridge that looked out over a peaceful lagoon with small islands dotted about it.

'I love this view,' he said. 'You're looking down at the centre of Port Vila, and out over a few of the smaller islands. Some of the other islands in the group are much larger than this one, but Vila, or Port Vila, the proper name, is the capital.'

He continued his tourist guide talk as they walked, pointing out the smart parliament building, telling her of the cyclone that had hit just east of the town a few years back, and the earthquakes the island group had suffered recently.

'Yet people still live here—they rebuild and life goes on?'

She turned towards him as she spoke, obviously intrigued.

'It is their home,' he reminded her, and she nodded.

'Of course it is.'

'And your home? Has it always been in Sydney?'

Normal, getting to know you talk, yet it felt more than that. Something inside him wanted to know more of this woman who'd come into his life.

'Always Sydney,' she replied.

They were heading downhill now, traffic thickening on the road as they came closer to the waterfront.

'And you?' she asked, moving closer to him as they passed a group of riotous holiday makers.

'Sydney, then a little town on the coast, Wetherby, then Sydney again. It's complicated.'

She smiled at him.

'Like the pelican?' she teased. 'Seems you'll have a lot to tell me over dinner.'

Was she interested or just being polite?

Not that it mattered. He might be attracted to this woman but everything about her told him she wasn't a candidate for a mutually enjoyable affair and anything more than that was still a little way down his 'to-do' list.

Not far down but still...

He returned to tour guide mode, pointing out various buildings, and soon they were down at the waterfront, and she stopped, looking out over the shining water.

'It's a beautiful setting for a town, isn't it?'

'It is indeed,' he agreed. 'It's one of the reasons I never mind coming back here.'

'The people being another?' she said, and he turned towards her and smiled.

'Of course!'

He led the way along the boardwalk built out over the water's edge towards the restaurant in a quieter part of the harbour. But a cry made them both turn. A group of Japanese tourists was talking excitedly and pointing down into the water, crowding so closely to the edge they were in danger of falling in.

Steve ran back, Fran following more slowly, arriving in time to catch Steve's shirt as he threw it off and stepped out of his sandals, before diving into the inky depths beneath them.

'Ambulance!' he yelled when he resurfaced, before diving back down out of sight.

Fran turned to one of the locals who'd joined the group, and said, 'Ambulance?'

He nodded, holding up his cell phone to show he was already on it.

Which left Fran free to push back the excited onlookers and beckon the burly local who'd phoned the ambulance to come and join her.

Steve's head reappeared, a very dark head beside it.

'If you can lean over, I think I can pass him up.'

The breathless words weren't quite as clear as they might have been, but Fran understood and she and the local man lay down so they could lean forward towards the water.

With what seemed like superhuman strength, Steve thrust the slight form of a young man upwards, to be grabbed by the stranger next to Fran, then Fran herself.

Together they hauled him up, with a couple from the tourist party helping to lift him clear. Fran waved the crowd away again and rested their patient in the recovery position, while Steve swam towards some steps fifty yards away.

Fran cleared the young man's airway and felt for a pulse. Not even a faint one!

Rolling him onto his back, she pinched his nose and gave five quick breaths, then changed position to begin chest compressions.

Steve arrived as she reached the count of thirty, so she let him take over the compressions while she counted and did the breaths. The ambulance siren was growing louder and louder as it neared them but they kept pumping and breathing until, finally, the young man gave a convulsive jerk, and Steve rolled him back into the recovery position before he brought up what seemed like a gallon of sea water.

He was breathing on his own, though still coughing and spluttering, when the ambos arrived to take over.

Fran and Steve stood together as the lad was strapped onto a gurney and loaded into the ambulance, and it was only when his shorts brushed against her that she realised he was still wet.

And somewhere in the chaos she'd lost his shirt.

Fortunately a backpacker appeared, holding the shirt and Steve's sandals.

'You two made a good team,' he said. 'No panic and straight into action. Done it before?'

Steve shook his head.

'Instinct,' he explained.

'And a bit of medical knowledge,' Fran added, feeling unaccountably pleased by the young man's words.

After handing over the shirt and sandals, the backpacker offered Steve a pair of board shorts.

'Might not be your style, mate, but better dry than wet,' he said cheerfully. 'You can keep them. I'm heading home and I could use a bit more space in my backpack.'

Obviously pleased by the offer, Steve stripped off his wet shorts, revealing a pair of lurid boxer shorts.

'Staff joke,' he explained as he pulled the dry shorts over them, then finished dressing with his shirt and sandals.

He turned to Fran, his arms out held.

'So, teammate, I might not be quite the picture of sartorial excellence you expected to be dining with, but will I do?'

'Definitely!' she said, then wondered why she felt there'd been a double meaning in her answer.

They finished the walk to the restaurant in companionable silence as if their brief response to the young man's drowning had somehow drawn them together.

'This is wonderful,' she said, as the waiter seated them at an outside table. 'And across there?'

She pointed to a small island with a row of thatched huts along the water's edge.

What she'd really wanted to know was how the young man might be faring, but common sense told her to leave that little interlude alone and not to make too much of it.

'One of many resorts,' he explained. 'Vanuatu's a tourist destination now. But that island over there, tiny as it is, has been settled for a long time. One of the colonial governors had a house there, and bits of it remain.'

'And it's only accessed by boat?'

Steve nodded. 'Look, the little boat is crossing now. It's about a five-minute trip but it does make that resort seem a bit special.'

A waiter interrupted them with menus and offers of drinks.

'Light beer for me,' Steve said. 'Fran?'

'I'd like a white wine, just a glass,' she told the waiter, who then rattled off a list of choices.

'Pinot Gris,' she said, getting lost after that in the list. And by the time their drinks arrived, they'd settled on their meals—steak for Steve and swordfish for Fran.

'Cheers,' he said, lifting his glass. 'And here's to a pleasant stay for you in Vanuatu. Hopefully you won't be called upon to save any more lives, although I must say you handled the situation enormously well.'

'Anyone would have done the same,' she said, ever so casually, although the compliment pleased her.

She touched her glass to his bottle, and echoed his 'Cheers' then took a sip of the wine, and nodded appreciation.

It was all Fran could do not to gulp at the wine.

Somehow, it seemed, the simple act of working together to save the young man had formed a bond between them.

Or maybe that was just her imagination! Running riot because the walk to the restaurant had set her nerves on fire?

The walk had certainly been fascinating, Steve pointing out special places, telling stories of the early European settlement, but it had been his presence—the nearness of him as they'd walked side by side—that had unsettled nerves she'd forgotten she had.

Oh, she'd been out with other men since her divorce, but none of them had made something—excitement—thrum along her nerves.

Maybe there was something in the richly perfumed tropical air—a drug of some kind—that heightened all the senses.

Or maybe seeing his broad, tanned chest, water nestling among the sparse hairs on his sternum, had stirred long-forgotten lust!

Or maybe she was just tired.

That was the most logical explanation for all these weird fancies...

But she didn't feel tired! She felt...alive.

'So, tell me about the pelican,' she said, to take her mind off nerves and feelings.

Steve grinned at her and she realised her question hadn't entirely worked because her nerves twitched in response to that grin.

'Local people know we're a clinic, but because we're not part of the hospital, they're not entirely sure what we do. Consequently, stories get around. We've had people calling in for physiotherapy and even marital counselling, but the pelican was a first.'

A real smile this time lit up his dark eyes, and pressed little smile lines into the corners of them.

'These two boys, about ten, I'd say, arrived dragging their go-cart behind them.'

He paused.

'You know go-carts—little boxy things on wheels that kids build themselves? They're great here because of the hills, though how some of them haven't been killed I don't know.'

'If they're going down a hill like the one we walked down, with the traffic, it would be suicidal. But anyway I know go-carts or at least the theory of them.'

'So the kids had this pelican in their go-cart. They'd found it near their home not far from the waterfront, and it appeared to have been hit by something—maybe a car. It had an injured leg and wing on one side and obviously couldn't fly and possibly couldn't walk as it sat quite contentedly in the cart.'

'And you don't do pelicans at the clinic?' Fran teased, drawn into the story by Steve's obvious involvement with the boys and the bird.

He smiled again, and she refused to acknowledge her physical reaction.

Perhaps she *was* tired.

'The problem was that the vet's place is half-way round the island and although it's only a small island, it was too far for the boys to drag their cart.'

'So you offered them a lift?'

He nodded.

'Put them, the cart and the bird in the old vehicle and probably broke any number of road rules getting them there so I could get back to the airport to meet you.'

Their meals arrived and their conversation paused, pleasing Fran as it gave her the opportunity to study the man across the table from her.

Surreptitiously, of course...

He was good-looking, though not in a plastic film-star kind of way—more manly, somehow, with good facial bones and strong features.

Tanned, but of course working here for several months of the year would ensure a year-round tan, with a few flecks of grey appearing in his dark hair. Just strands, here and there, though they obviously didn't bother him.

But it was his smile, even his half-smile, quirking up at one corner of his mouth that sent the tingles down her spine.

Oh, for heaven's sake, you've just met the man, and you don't believe in love at first sight.

Not that it was love, only attraction.

But she didn't believe in that either...

'So, growing up?' she said, deciding talking was far better than mulling over her reactions to the man. 'Sydney, and you mentioned...?'

'Wetherby!'

He said it as if the place was special to him, so she pursued it, wanting to keep a conversation going, but also wanting to know more about this man who had set up a clinic in this place and drove small boys and pelicans to vets.

'Wetherby?' she said.

Steve knew what she was asking, but did she really want to know?

And did he really want to talk about his childhood?

Usually not, but with *this* woman?

Maybe.

'Wetherby is a very small coastal town where, as one of my foster sisters always said, nothing ever happens.'

'Foster sisters?'

'My parents died when I was eight.'

Memories of that time flicked across his mind like images on a screen. The sheer disbelief that suddenly he didn't have his beloved mother, his laughing, boisterous father...

'How terrible for you.'

He looked at Fran across the table and knew she'd meant it. She'd known pain herself, he'd read it in her eyes earlier today, when they'd been discussing the IVM...

'It was hard. I'd been left with my nanny while they flew to America, to get me, they'd said, a brother or sister. At that age America is the place where movies come from so it seemed perfectly reasonable that you could pick up a child there as well. It was only later, with Hallie's help, that I pieced it all together.'

'Hallie?'

They'd finished their meals and pushed their plates to the side, and Fran was watching him over her glass as she sipped at the last of the wine.

'There was a foster home in Wetherby, and I honestly believe I won the jackpot, being sent there. Hallie was the housemother—Hallie and her husband Pop ran the place and somehow melded a mob of very divergent types into a family.'

Fran was frowning at him now, but no less lovely when she frowned.

'Had you no relation who would take you?' she asked, and he pulled his mind from his companion to go on, feeling a need to explain.

'I was the only child of only children, and it was because they'd both hated being only children that my parents were going to the US. IVF was fairly well established here but whatever problem my mother had, had prevented it working for her. My father flew so it must have seemed the natural thing for them to do—head off in search of someone who might help.'

'Such desperation,' Fran said quietly, 'but at least they both wanted the child they were seeking.'

He studied her for a moment, sure there was something behind the words, but before he could ask, she'd prompted him again.

'Go on.'

The gentleness in her tone led him back to the past.

'To answer your first question, I did have relations—I had a grandmother, my father's mother, and a grandfather on my mother's side—but neither of them were really capable of looking after me, even with the nanny. The obvious answer, to them, was boarding school.'

'At eight?' Fran queried, and Steve's answering nod told her it had not been good.

'I hated it,' he said simply. 'Fortunately, a close friend of my mother's saw the state I was in, and arranged for me to go into foster care, with the proviso I spend my Christmas holidays with my grandparents. They lived in adjacent houses, my parents having grown up together, and both of them had housekeepers who could look after me for the short time I was with them.

'But Wetherby was where you spent most of your time?'

'I lived there until I left to go to university, by which time my grandfather had died and my grandmother had gone into a nursing home. I sold my grandfather's house and bought an apartment in Sydney.'

'But kept the other house?'

He grinned at her.

'Well, the house was still my grandmother's, but it was also the house where I'd lived with my parents. It is a house made for a family, and I knew that's what I eventually wanted, so even after my grandmother died I kept it, and leased it out until I needed it.'

'And you need it now? You live there? With your family?'

'No family yet,' he told her, 'but, yes, I live there.'

'So you've come home,' she said, smiling at him, making all the attraction he'd felt from the moment he'd first seen her come rushing back to life within his body.

Really, this was just too much.

It was madness.

They were both here to work.

Holiday romance?

Even as the words whispered in his head he knew that wouldn't work.

Not with this woman.

She was, as Hallie would have said, a keeper. Although the first woman he'd thought had been a keeper had thrown his engagement ring at him and disappeared from his life.

Then and there, he'd decided to work through his list and wait until he'd achieved it all before he settled down with marriage and children. He smiled as he thought of that list, the original now so tattered he'd had to paste it into a book to prevent its total disintegration.

'Happy thoughts?' Fran asked, and he realised she'd caught the smile.

'More nostalgia,' he said. 'I was thinking about a list I wrote a long time ago.'

'A list?'

'Hallie knew just how lost I was when I arrived in Wetherby. One day she sat me down and said that what I'd been through was terrible, but that I couldn't live in the past. I needed to think about what I wanted for the future and to live for that.'

'Big job for, what—an eight-year-old?'

'I was ten by then, but it did make me think seriously about what I wanted. Unfortunately, all I could come up with was a family and that wasn't exactly possible right then. I talked to Hallie and she told me that anything was possible, that I just had to work out how to make it happen. She asked me, "Where would you start?"'

He could hear Hallie's voice in his head as clear as if the conversation had been yesterday.

'"With growing up?" I suggested, and I can see her smiling now. She found a piece of paper and told me to write it down, all the steps I'd need to take to get to growing up, so I wrote, "Finish school," and next I put, "Go to university, then get to be an IVF doctor—"'

'Ambition to be an IVF doctor at ten?' Fran

asked, and he had to smile at the disbelief in her voice. 'Oh, because of your parents. Of course!'

She reached out and touched his hand where it was resting on the table, a touch that offered sympathy and understanding. It was all he could do not to turn it up and wrap this fingers around hers, but knew that would only confuse matters.

'So, at ten you decided to specialise in IVF without any idea of what that might entail.'

He grinned at her.

'Hallie helped out there, so I wrote down to study medicine, specialise in O and G *then* be an IVF doctor.'

'And was that the end of your list?'

'Of course not,' he said, enjoying this confession now. 'I was the only child of only children so it was natural that the last thing on the list—the ultimate goal—was to get married and have a heap of children. Hallie helped there too, explaining that children cost money, and getting established in a profession would take time and also cost money, so there were incidentals in the list before it got to the marriage and children.'

So forget all about attraction to this man, Fran told herself. With his list-driven ambitions he would already have the wife picked out.

'You must be nearly there,' she said, shaking her head at the dessert menu the waiter was offering her. 'Did your list specify a particular woman?'

He laughed.

'No, I didn't get that specific, although at ten I was madly in love with one of my stepsisters, Liane.'

'And are you looking for someone like Liane?'

Fran knew she shouldn't be pursuing this. Steve's future marriage—his whole life—was nothing to do with her. *Nothing!* It had to be the inexplicable attraction going on inside her that had her probing like this.

'There is no one like Liane,' he said, and the look of sorrow on his face told her more firmly than the words that the conversation was finished.

They left the restaurant, Steve explaining that, although they never took advantage of it, the restaurant refused to charge the clinic workers for their meals.

'It's their contribution to what we do,' he explained, as he took her elbow to walk back to the path along the harbour.

They paused near the little jetty where the boat crossed to the island resort and she looked around, appreciating this magical place through all her senses—the sight of the moon on the water, the competing aromas of flowers and sea and suntan lotion, the sound of the waves lapping against the beach, and the feel of the slightly damp tropical air brushing against her skin.

'It's beautiful.'

The words came out on a sigh, as she realised how constrained her life had been—how ordinary she'd made it—hurting after the divorce and retreating into the humdrum of everyday existence when she could have been here—or anywhere—helping others as Steve was doing, or simply enjoying carefree holidays.

Steve could have echoed the words, but he would have meant her—standing there, looking out to sea, the breeze blowing the fine material of her dress against her body, silhouetting her against the sky.

Her hair lifted softly around her face, and her skin seemed luminous in the moonlight.

Was it her beauty that had prompted him to pour out his life story to her over dinner?

He'd probably bored her rigid.

Yet somehow he felt she'd understood—that she'd suffered pain herself...

He wanted to ask her—about her life, about herself—but dinner had gone on longer than he'd expected and by the time they climbed the hill it would be late.

He hailed a cab.

'I could have walked,' she protested, as he held the door for her.

'And arrived back all hot and sweaty. Not to-night, when you've just arrived and haven't ac-climatised. Besides, my wet boxers are chaffing,' he added with a laugh.

'Next time I'll walk,' she said firmly, and he hoped there would be a next time.

Now, why on earth had she said that? Fran wondered, as she rode back up the hill beside Steve.

As if the physical attraction between them wasn't enough, listening to him, hearing the pain he must have suffered lying behind his careful words, seeing the orphaned boy in her mind, she'd felt emotional attraction, which, she rather thought, would be far more dangerous than the physical stuff.

Harder to fight…

The ride was short, and she had to smile when, as they walked down to their accommodation, Steve said, 'Well, you've only yourself to blame for me pouring out my life story to you. You did ask. But mind, it will be your turn tomorrow— fair's fair!'

'My life story?' she said. 'Compared to yours it is as bland and predictable as milk—it could be summed up in about two lines. Was born, grew up, became an embryologist, got married, got divorced, still working as an embryologist.'

'Aha,' he said, as they reached her door, 'that's a very teasing summation. Tomorrow night we'll start with the "became an embryologist". Most people don't head off to university with that as an aim.'

'No, I studied science but liked the little bit of embryology I did in my set course, so pursued it.'

She looked at him, aware of his body close to hers, but hyper-aware that he was studying her face.

Searching for more information behind her words?

Or something else?

'Thank you for everything,' she said, because the longer they stood there the more she wanted to touch him. She stepped back, putting more space between them. 'Not only for dinner, but for bringing me here.'

She wanted to tell him that even after less than twenty-four hours in this magical place she felt her life had changed. But he'd think she was mad or, worse, wonder about her life back home that such a short time here could mean so much.

So she said goodnight and slipped inside her

door, poking her head back out to say, 'Okay if I use the bathroom first?'

He was still standing where she'd left him, and he nodded but didn't move, his face puzzled as if he, too, felt something had happened between them.

Fran lay in bed the following morning, remembering all she'd learned about the man with whom she was working. She'd seen a little of the island, magical in the moonlight as well, but it had been the scrap of Steve's history—heavily edited, she guessed—that had caught and held her imagination.

She could even picture him as a young child, chewing at his pencil, as he made up his list.

And realising just how dedicated he had been, and no doubt still was, to that list, then she should forget about all the physical attraction she'd been feeling towards him.

Well aware that brief affairs or holiday romances weren't for her, she'd just have to steer clear of any opportunity for closeness between them.

Sure, she had to work with him, but that was work and if she gave it her full concentration, surely she wouldn't feel all the tingling awareness his presence was already causing her.

Thinking work, which had kept her going through all the trials and tribulations of the divorce, would surely get her back to normal!

Unable to sleep, Steve left for his run earlier than usual. The streetlights were still on, although dawn was breaking, the orange blaze in the eastern sky already heralding the rising sun.

Why, in the name of fortune, had he poured out his heart to Fran last night?

Well, not his heart but his life story—more or less. Telling her about Wetherby, Hallie and Pop, Liane even. He never talked to anyone about Liane...

His feet pounded faster, and he could feel sweat breaking out all over his body.

If he cut short his run, he could be back in time to have breakfast with Fran.

Really, he should go back.

Nonsense, he rarely had breakfast with other visiting staff, just grabbed whatever was to hand when he came back from his run, or breakfasted at the hospital to catch up with the news there.

But she was new...

Or was it because he was attracted to her that he suddenly wanted to see her?

See her over breakfast...

That was worse because surely seeing someone over breakfast was—what—intimate?

Give me a break!

But without consciously realising it, he'd turned back towards the clinic.

Why shouldn't he have breakfast with her?

CHAPTER THREE

THANKFULLY SHE WAS out of the bathroom when he got back, so he showered and shaved, slipped into some respectable 'work' clothes—which here meant shirt and shorts—and found the woman who'd broken his running schedule sitting at the table, where, as usual, Zoe had laid out a variety of cereals, fruit, yoghurt and freshly baked pastries.

'The pastries are delicious,' Fran said as he joined her.

She looked cool and together in the same uniform as him—shirt and shorts, sandals, he suspected, on her feet.

Was he considering her clothes so that he didn't have to think about his physical reactions to the sight of her? Physical reactions he had never felt towards a virtual stranger.

Although, why shouldn't he be attracted to her? She had told him last night that she was divorced.

Though surely someone so lovely would already have another significant other...

'Good morning,' he said, settling opposite her, serving himself some cereal and fruit while his mind put his body firmly into place.

They were here to work!

'I like the couples to meet the whole team,' Steve began. 'It's easier to have the embryologist there in case they have questions. Our first couple is due at ten but island time is fairly flexible.'

She glanced up at him and he noticed a tiny flake of pastry on the corner of her lip.

He clutched his spoon tightly to stop himself from reaching out to brush it away, and prayed his colleague wasn't reading his body language.

'If you think it's important I'll be there,' Fran assured him, speaking coolly, formally, as if determined to steer away from the easy camaraderie they'd shared the previous evening.

After which she pushed her chair back, excused

herself, and left, no doubt to remove the crumb of pastry herself.

Which was a good thing, wasn't it?

Well?

On one side, keeping things cool and professional between them was certainly the way he worked with colleagues at home, especially after the hash he'd made of his relationship with Sally. Their break-up had lost him friends and had forced him into setting up his own clinic sooner than he'd intended.

Here, with the small team, they were naturally close, becoming friends as well as colleagues, but no more than friends.

On the other hand…

He didn't really want to think about the other hand. About the fact that this might be the very woman with whom he could have his family.

He half smiled at the thought of Liane hearing him say this.

Forget the bloody family and choose a woman because you love her, she would have said.

But physical attraction wasn't love…

* * *

Mr and Mrs Red were the first of the couples they saw, coming in concerned, anxiety throbbing from them both as Steve ran through the procedures.

He did his best to help them relax, talking with Mr Red about the sperm sample they would need, explaining how they liked to take that first so he could be with Mrs Red when they extracted any eggs she might have.

The two tall, well-built islanders clung to each other like children, their handsome faces drawn with stress. And for all that she hadn't wanted to be there, it was the client's stress that prompted Fran to intrude in what should be Steve's part of the procedure, inserting herself into the conversation.

'Nothing makes it easier,' she told them in a gentle voice, 'so you just have to think of something you really hate, like going to the dentist, and realise that soon it will all be over.'

Mr and Mrs Red seemed to take that in, and they were soon reassuring her that they didn't mind at all, and the stiffness in the atmosphere melted away. Mr Red kissed his wife goodbye before being led off to a little room, after which Fran followed Steve as he took Mrs Red into the procedure room where he introduced her to Alex, the permanent doctor at the clinic.

'Alex tells us you have some lovely eggs ready for collection,' Steve said to Mrs Red. 'I want to have a look at them, then we'll give you a light sedative so you won't feel any pain and when your husband comes back we can collect them. Francesca is here to take care of them from the moment we get them.'

'Kind of like an egg midwife or perhaps a clucky hen,' she put in, because Mrs Red was looking distressed again. 'Believe me, no one will take better care of them than me.'

She took the woman's hand and gave the fingers a reassuring squeeze. Okay, she'd crossed the boundaries between doctor and embryologist and probably stepped on Steve's toes. But suddenly none of her need for restraint and remaining distant from the patient mattered as long as

Mrs Red was as comfortable as she could be while they messed around with her body.

The ultrasound, operated by Alex, showed a number of follicles beautifully swollen, indicating that several eggs might be ready for collection. Mr Red came into the procedure room, smiling with relief that he'd done his part in the procedure. He took Fran's place by his wife's side as Alex sedated the woman and Steve used the ultrasound to guide him to her ovaries and draw up fluid from the ripe follicles.

Fran had her red-marked dish ready for the fluid Steve would collect and held it for him as he released it from the fine syringe. She carried it down to the laboratory, peering at it under the microscope, separating out four fine eggs and transferring them carefully into separate red-marked dishes, these with the special culture in them—fluid that would nurture the eggs while they were outside Mrs Red's body.

It was science, nothing more, she tried to tell herself, but somehow, in this magical place, it had become more personal.

Because she'd been shocked back into feeling by her attraction to Steve? Not that that was going anywhere…

But in spite of that, this day was unlike any other she'd ever spent in a lab; all her senses on full alert, excitement stirring within her.

She put the eggs in the incubator and turned her attention to Mr Red's sample, which had to be washed and examined for any problems or impurities.

'Well, you're feisty little buggers,' she was saying happily to the sperm when Steve walked into the lab.

'Do you always talk to your specimens?' he asked, and she tried to feel embarrassed but found she couldn't.

'Not usually,' she admitted 'but today I'm just happy that they look good and the eggs are good, too,' she added, refusing to have her positive mood dampened by this man. He might have tipped her world off course by making her feel again, but she quite liked the new direction it had taken and she was going to go with it.

'Actually,' she added, 'I do so little practical work these days, mainly supervising the younger embryologists, that I'm excited about this.'

There was no understanding smile.

Nothing!

Oh, well…

'I'm sorry if I intruded when I shouldn't have earlier but they both seemed so stressed.'

'Don't apologise. You managed to get them relaxed, which was wonderful. And we're a team, we work together for the best outcomes we can for the patients. Now, ready to go again? Mr and Mrs Utai are here.'

'Yellow.' Fran responded. 'I'll make them yellow.' She didn't add that she'd call them that, he'd think she was even more peculiar than he'd thought when he heard her talking to her specimen.

Steve watched as she put into the incubator the red dish she'd been examining when he'd come in, then break open the yellow pack. He liked that she was so organised—not that he'd doubted she would be. Right from their first meeting she'd given the impression of smooth efficiency.

Yet he'd glimpsed something of the woman underneath that polished exterior as she'd talked to the previous patients, empathising with them in a way he couldn't, winning their confidence with a few light-hearted comments.

He was intrigued, which wasn't good. Attraction was all very well, and *it* had reached a stage of undeniability, given the way his body was behaving in her presence, but to be interested in her as a person, that was different.

Patients awaited. He'd concentrate on them and think about his colleague later.

Or not think about her later—that would be a better idea.

'Done, done, done!'

It was late afternoon as Fran did a little dance in front of the incubator after she'd checked both the red and the yellow dishes, now with the sperm added to them, and tucked them back into the warm atmosphere they needed to meet and match.

She had no idea why she was feeling so positive about both couples but she was, although now her work was done for the day, she knew let-down could sneak in if she let it. Her own experiences had been so negative it was hard to stay positive, but in this magical place with the gentle, beautiful people, surely nothing could go wrong.

Steve came in as she was tidying the benches and setting out the coloured packs for the patients they'd see the next day.

'All done?' he asked, and she nodded, pleased she still felt positive enough to smile.

'You really like this work?' he queried, picking up on the smile.

'Don't you?' she challenged.

He frowned at her, then finally replied, 'Most of the time.'

'The failures?' she guessed, coming closer and reaching out to touch his hand, wanting to reassure him as she'd reassured the Reds earlier. 'They are not your fault. Everyone accepts that the medical team does the best they can. Everyone going into IVF understands the facts and figures, the chances of success and the even bigger chances of failure. They go because it *is* a chance and it's the doctors and their teams who are giving them that chance.'

He was still frowning, but she sensed it was a different kind of frown, so when he said, 'You're not really who you portray yourself as, are you?' she kind of understood and smiled at him.

'I think I was, but something's changed,' she told him, then she reached up and let her hair out of its restraining band, shaking her head to let her hair fly free. 'Must be the hang-loose thing,' she added, although inside the old her was quivering with shock at this behaviour. She'd not only stripped off her outer shell but she was admitting it to a man she barely knew.

'Good,' Steve said, although the loose hair and bright smile had made him forget the cool and professional thing. 'Because now we're done for the day and I thought I'd take you for a drive to see something of the island. While Vila is the main town there are small settlements on the other side with farmland and beautiful beaches.

'I'd love that!' she said, her smile even brighter. 'Can you give me a few minutes for a quick shower?' She was peeling off her lab coat as she spoke, dumping it in the laundry bin, which Akila would collect later.

'We've plenty of time,' he assured her, and walked with her down to their quarters.

But his mind was playing with the words. Plenty of time—for what?

She was here for a month—a lifetime in a lot of affairs…

Not that he was thinking of an affair.

Was he?

She was true to her word, reappearing five minutes later, looking fresh and trim in clean shorts and a blue-green shirt that matched her eyes.

They climbed into the trusty four-wheel drive and Steve headed down through the town then turned south, pointing out resort after resort, until they turned off the main highway onto a road that wound through rainforest with patches of cleared farmland.

It was pleasant doing a sightseeing tour of the island, Fran thought, except that it put her in very close proximity to the man who was causing her body so many problems.

Then the view opened up before her, dark blue ocean stretching away to the horizon.

'Oh, that is so beautiful,' she murmured, forgetting the discomfort of his proximity as she took in the small waves breaking against the white sand of the beach. 'And so quiet after the bustle of Vila.'

They dropped down onto the flat where the ocean was now only visible through a fringe of palm trees.

'Look, there are pigs.'

Steve was smiling, no doubt at her startled remark.

'Don't see many pigs where you live?' he teased, and she smiled too.

'Not poking around in the sandy dirt right beside the road,' she retorted, and the thread of tension she'd felt when she'd first joined him in the vehicle disappeared completely.

He stopped in a small, deserted car park.

'We're on the eastern side of the island now—or maybe south-eastern—and this is Eton, the water called Banana Bay. This place would be jumping if the surf was up, but the winds are wrong for surfing here at this time of the year.'

He turned to look at her, wanting to look at her.

Wanting more?

'Care to walk along the beach?'

'Care to walk along a deserted beach, fringed by palm trees, with crystal-clear water to paddle in? Who wouldn't?'

She was out of the car in an instant, bending to take off her sandals then throw them back into the footwell.

'Race you to the water!'

He let her win.

Of course he let her win—he was too busy watching the joy he could read in her movements to do more than follow slowly.

She kicked one foot into the tide, sending a

rainbow of droplets into the air as the setting sun caught them with its rays, and, watching her, Steve wondered if what he felt was love.

Couldn't possibly be, his sensible self assured him. Heartburn was a far more likely explanation for the tightness in his chest.

He joined her in the shallow water, splashing beside her as they strolled aimlessly along, until she stopped and turned to him, taking one of his hands in both of hers.

'I want to thank you,' she said, her eyes as serious as the tone of her voice, 'for bringing me here. I know I've only begun the work I'm doing with you, but already I know this is the best thing I've ever done.'

She paused and he wondered if she was searching for the words she needed, or if she was considering whether or not to say them.

Possibly the latter, he realised, as she added, 'I feel alive again.'

Trusting blue-green eyes looked into his.

'Truly alive. Hanging loose!'

There had to be something behind such an admission, something bad that had happened in her past, but right now it didn't matter what it was.

He reached out and put his hand on her neck, just beneath her hair.

'And just how loose are you hanging?' he asked quietly.

Fran studied him, suddenly all out of words. She'd gone too far—way too far. In fact, she was so far out of her comfort zone she had no idea how to proceed.

'I'm not entirely sure,' she admitted, but as the hand he'd tucked under her hair drew her closer, she suspected she was about to find out.

It was just a kiss, nothing more, or so she told herself as his lips met hers, but whatever rebellion against restraint that had already begun in her head was infecting her body as well, and she found herself responding, kissing him back, giving all the excited nerves free rein.

Just when she began to tremble she wasn't sure, but Steve must have felt it for he lifted his head and held her shoulders, looking down into her face.

'Okay?' he asked, dark eyes she could drown in looking deep into hers, an emotion she couldn't read making them appear even darker.

Beyond words, she nodded, wondering just where the conversation would go next, realising how little experience she'd had with men. It had always been Nigel, right from high school, and as far as she could remember, Nigel's kisses hadn't made her tremble.

Maybe they had at the beginning...

And after they'd separated, there'd been the odd date, usually set up by well-meaning friends, but although all the men she'd met were fine, there'd been no magic, and definitely no tremble-inducing kisses.

No deep connection that might have led to love.

Love?

When had love come into it?

But Steve was kissing her again and it was all she could do to keep upright, let alone answer questions!

This next kiss seared her skin, heat building within her as well. She clung to Steve, had to for support, and as his tongue probed her lips her mouth opened on a sigh, and she tasted him, teased his teasing tongue with her own, her hands around his neck now, holding his head to hers, while his arms held her close enough for her to know exactly how he felt.

A barking dog broke them apart, and they turned to see a black 'bitsa' lolloping down the beach towards them, an elderly islander well behind him.

Steve bent to scratch the dog behind its ears, talking quietly to it, while Fran stared at the man who seemed, with a kiss—well, two kisses—to have changed the direction of her life.

She'd always been a 'good' girl, and her husband had been her only lover. But Nigel's kisses had never made her want to strip off on a beach and make love on the sand.

Wild passionate love, given the heat of the kiss—kisses…

The islander was closer now, calling out a greeting.

Fran waved to him, then wandered back into

the shallow water, splashing again, letting her body cool, while her mind churned with memories of heat and a dozen 'what-ifs'.

Steve spoke to the man, the language almost English but not quite. She recognised a little French and some native tongue mixed in.

'Bislama, the language spoken here,' Steve explained as the man and dog continued along the beach. 'It's a kind of hybrid pidgin English.'

'And you speak it?' Fran asked, studying this man who was full of surprises.

'A little,' he admitted. Then, with a smile that made her toes curl, he added, 'I couldn't have explained what we were doing on the beach but I suppose he guessed that!'

Fran could only stare at him, more unsure of herself than she'd ever been.

Steve read the shadows in her eyes—uncertainty, vulnerability, and perhaps a hint of fear as well.

Not that he wasn't totally thrown by the situation himself...

He took her hand so they could walk together.

'I don't normally kiss my embryologists,' he said, running his thumb across the soft skin on her hand.

She glanced up at him, looking worried now, so he smiled and added, 'And that's not because they've nearly always been men.'

Her low throaty chuckle made his body squirm with desire, but he'd chased away the shadows in her eyes.

'I'm not much of a casual kisser myself,' she said, and it was his turn to laugh.

Certain there was nothing more to say, not now anyway, he slipped an arm around her waist and was pleased when she did the same to him, so they could walk arm in arm along the beach, the setting sun turning the water into a sheet of pink that deepened to purple as the sun sank over the hill behind them.

'Best get back to the car before it's dark. Night comes quickly here,' he said, turning her around and wandering up across the dry sand towards the coconut palms.

'Tell me about yourself,' he said, when they were on the road back to the clinic again.

'I told you yesterday,' she replied. 'I've led a very dull, predictable life. But what of you—your real family—what were they like?'

Steve hesitated, then realised just how little he'd ever told anyone about his family. Maybe talking to Fran would help him sort out his muddled thoughts about his early childhood.

'I never knew my parents well—perhaps no child does at eight. Maybe it's only later we put the bits and pieces together and see them as real people, but I didn't get that chance.'

He paused, searching for words to explain.

'They were fun, I know that. They had parties and I'd watch from the top of the stairs, see them laughing, sometimes dancing, always crowds of people around them.'

He tried to think back.

'They loved me, I'm sure of that, although they travelled a lot, something to do with family businesses, both my father's and my mother's family businesses. And I had a nanny who mostly looked after me. But when they were home, they always read my bedtime story, and tucked me in, and kissed me goodnight.'

Fran heard the words with a little ache in her heart. She didn't consider herself as having had a storybook childhood, even after her father had left them when she was five. But she had loads more memories of her parents than simply ones of people who kissed her goodnight.

And she'd had grandparents and cousins and memories of Christmas with the whole family gathered, twenty or thirty adults and children all eating roast turkey on a broiling hot summer's day.

She slid her hand across to rest on Steve's knee, giving it a little squeeze of encouragement.

'Go on,' she prompted.

'I think I told you they were both only children. They'd grown up next door to each other, in big houses overlooking the harbour.'

'Plenty of money.' It was a statement, not a question, and Steve nodded his agreement.

'It's how I've been able to start this clinic, and some other ventures back at home.'

But money can't buy love, or so they say, Fran thought, understanding now Steve's strong desire for a family of his own—something he'd never actually had.

Relations, yes, but a family?

'You were lucky with your foster home,' she said, realising where his knowledge of what a family could be like came from.

'I was,' he said. 'Luckier than anyone would believe.'

He turned towards her and smiled.

'Why else would I have family at the top of my to-do list? Well, literally, it's at the bottom but it's the ultimate goal.'

Fran pasted a smile on her face, although inside she could feel the pain of what could never be.

Stupid really, to have connected to this man on the basis of two kisses, but connect she had.

Closely!

And, no, it couldn't possibly be love—love had to be nurtured, grown from small beginnings.

Didn't it?

Whatever! This man was not for her.

Except?

Just for here?

An affair?

Could she handle that?

The trembling began again, although her mind was more steadfast.

Good grief, of course she could. She was a mature woman, already married and divorced, and if she'd managed a father who'd deserted her, and a mother who never seemed to have recovered from the desertion, plus three failed cycles of IVF, *and* the advent of Clarissa into Nigel's life, without completely cracking up, she could handle anything!

They were on the road up to the clinic now, quiet at this time of the evening, and Steve had lifted one hand off the steering wheel to cover hers where it lay on his knee.

'That was great,' he said. 'We'll have to do it again.'

The kissing?

Perhaps she could handle anything but uncertainty.

'The drive part or the beach part?' she asked as they pulled up by the huge bougainvillea.

His frown told her she'd lost him, but as his eyes searched her face, the frown was replaced by a smile.

'Both,' he said firmly. 'But definitely the beach part.'

He used the hand that still held hers to draw her closer, and brushed his lips across hers, sending tremors of need through her body.

But before she could respond he'd drawn back, getting out of the car and coming around to help her out, smiling at her as if something had been settled, though what, she had no idea.

'I've got to see Alex about something but will see you for dinner,' he said, squeezing her fingers before releasing them.

How she got back to their lodging with her knees shaking so much, Fran didn't know, but she *did* make it.

She pressed her hands to her cheeks, feeling the

heat in them for all she didn't blush, then sank onto the bed, wondering what came next.

Should she say something? Indicate she'd be happy to have an affair with him?

Surely not, that would sound far too clinical!

Besides, it might not be what he wanted…

Perhaps, she decided as she stood up and gathered her toiletries, she'd leave it all to Steve. Undoubtedly he knew a whole lot more about flings, affairs and holiday romances than she did.

Probably about sex too!

The thought snuck into her head and she felt her cheeks grow hot again. Maybe she did know how to blush.

Unfortunately, checking out her wardrobe for something to put on after her shower brought her down to earth with a thud. Last night in the long blue dress she'd looked attractive enough to interest Steve, but as far as the rest of her clothes were concerned, that was it for soft and pretty. Everything else was strictly practical, tailored linen shorts and sensible shirts, not a flower or a floating panel in sight.

Disappointment rocketed through her body and although she told herself it was utterly stupid to want to look pretty for Steve and that at her age she should know better, the disappointment remained like a solid lump of ice in the middle of her chest.

Although...

What had Zoe said when she'd shown Fran around?

Something about muumuus in a bottom drawer of the dresser? People coming from different climates and often not having anything cool to wear?

Fran examined the dresser. She hadn't needed the bottom drawer so hadn't opened it, but now she did and gazed in wonder at the brightly flowered muumuus folded neatly in it. All new with tags—presumably people who used them took them home and paid to replace them, which is what she'd do, she decided, pulling out the least vibrant of them, a dusky blue with purple flowers—truly the least vibrant!

Could she wear it?

Wouldn't she look foolish?

She folded the garment and returned it to the drawer, her fear of looking foolish overcoming any stupid desire to look pretty for Steve, but even as his name sounded in her head, his voice came through the door.

'If you need something cool to put on after your shower, there is always a collection of muumuus in a bottom drawer.'

The spurt of what had to be jealousy that shot through her shocked her so much she knew she wouldn't wear any of the pretty garments. Although he *had* said he didn't usually kiss his embryologists so maybe he just knew about the garments rather than having any specific experience with them—or the women in them!

She headed for the bathroom only to find it in use, Steve obviously having decided she'd finished in there.

Totally lost now, ill at ease, and wondering what on earth she was getting herself into, she wandered out the back door, clutching her toiletries bag, clean undies, shirt and shorts, and blinked at the sight before her eyes.

Someone—surely not Steve—had spread flowers across the centre of the outdoor table, the barbecue lid was up and the coals beneath the grill plate were heating, while along the benches on both sides of the grill, banana leaves were spread with food—sliced vegetables, a whole fish, fruits she didn't recognise, the lot covered with a fine net to protect them from insects.

Could she really wear her shirt and shorts to such a feast?

If she was actually considering a fling with Steve, couldn't she go the whole way—wear the pretty muumuu?

But uncertainty still dogged her, the restraint she'd developed throughout her childhood brought on by the fear of losing her remaining parent, and then continuing in her marriage. *My colleagues, clients and friends expect the best of everything*, Nigel had always said, but nothing showy or obtrusive.

Until she felt arms circle her from behind, and Steve press a kiss on her shoulder.

'You're fretting about the kisses, aren't you? They don't have to lead anywhere, you know. We can be all grown-up and pretend to each other— denying the attraction that seems to have sprung up between us. Although I doubt it will go away. As far as you're concerned, I find you a very sexy woman, but the last thing I'd want, Francesca, is to push you into something you don't want.'

She turned in his arms and pressed her body against his, wanting him yet still uncertain, although as he kissed her again, this time just beneath her ear, the desire for him grew strong enough to chase away uncertainty.

'My friends call me Fran,' she said, giving in to the delight of his kisses which, now, were trailing down her neck.

'Fran or Francesca, you are delectably kissable,' he said, then he lifted his head, dropped a light kiss on her lips, turned her towards the house and patted her on the backside. 'Go shower while I cook or we'll never eat,' he said, making things sound so normal she trotted off to do as she was told, although when she dressed after the shower she did leave the top buttons of her shirt undone.

CHAPTER FOUR

'NO MUUMUU?' STEVE TEASED, then he shook his head. 'Actually, I think you're more of a sarong type.'

He disappeared into his room and returned with a rolled-up piece of material in dark blue with unlikely green hibiscus flowers on it.

'These are left for the men—they wear them tied around their waist, but it would fit you as a sarong, wrapped around and tied above the breasts. You could try it now, or for dinner tomorrow.'

The slight smile curling his lips suggested he was already imagining her in it, and though she was sure she never blushed, she was also sure her cheeks were heating.

'Thank you,' she managed. 'Maybe tomorrow.'

But just imagining the sarong, led to images

of Steve untying it, unwrapping her, and heat swamped her body.

She plonked down on a chair beside the table— one where she could watch him as he worked— wondering why this man, of all the men she'd met and worked with, could affect her as he did, sending her spinning right off her stable axis into the unknown.

Her mind whirled as she sought for answers, while her fingers idly picked up flowers from the central display, poking them randomly into her hair for something to do.

She looked at the sarong, and excitement skittered inside her, churning her stomach so badly she was sure she wouldn't be able to eat, when even her normally sensible brain was remembering beach kisses and wondering where they would lead.

Or perhaps that was her body talking...

She lifted a frangipani flower, creamy white with a vivid yellow centre, and breathed in the heady perfume. Tucked it in between her breasts, where the undone buttons showed just a hint of a deep cleavage.

Would Steve like her breasts?

The thought was foreign to her yet it brought warmth sweeping downward between her legs, and a heaviness that made the restraints of her bra uncomfortable.

The idea that she, sensible, practical Francesca Hawthorne, could be sitting lusting over an almost stranger was unfathomable, but that's certainly what was happening. She could feel the moisture gathering, her nipples pebbling, just thinking about what lay ahead...

Sensible, practical Francesca, however, did recover sufficiently to ask if there was anything she could do to help, but Steve only half turned and smiled at her, a warm, delighted kind of smile.

'Relax, that's what you can do. In fact, there might be something here to help with that.'

He reached into a cupboard under one of the side benches and held up a small bottle of beer.

'Beer, wine, something soft? The French influence spreads to alcohol here in Vanuatu so the wines are usually French and very good. A light, dry white perhaps?'

She nodded agreement then realised she could at least get it for herself and stood up, moving towards him, flowers falling from her hair as she did so.

Totally embarrassed, she raised her hands to pull them out, but he caught her hands.

'Hanging loose,' he reminded her, touching the frangipani nestled between her breasts. 'Remember?'

All right, so she *could* blush! She'd obviously not had any need for blushes before.

She bent and found the wine, together with some glasses, frosted with cold, but as Steve had already knocked the top off the beer, she pulled out only one, unscrewing the top off the wine—pleased screw-tops had become commonplace so she didn't have to fight a cork—and poured herself a glass of the pale liquid.

It was deliciously cold, and so refreshing she'd finished her glass before she realised it, and though tempted to pour another one, she waited, deciding to have one with her meal, determined not to look as if she needed the Dutch courage of alcohol to get her through whatever might lie ahead.

But thinking of what might lie ahead set her body on fire once again, so she poured another glass of wine, and a glass of cold water as well.

Was he always so aware of women he'd been kissing? Steve wondered. Or was it because Francesca—Fran—was so different from his usual women that he was hyper-aware of her? It was obvious she was feeling awkward and uncertain after what had happened at the beach and this knowledge made him feel very protective of her. Made him want to hug and reassure her, but touching her was dangerous.

So cooking for her, eating with her, became a kind of foreplay, unusual for him but no less tantalising for that.

The meal done, they sat at the table and talked of work, of experiences they'd had, Fran—yes, he liked the shortened version—proving a humorous conversationalist as well as an intelligent one.

She could joke about her lab work, which obviously fascinated her, and told stories of the things that had happened there, but she steered away from personal questions and he guessed for all her talk of happy family Christmases there'd been pain and disillusion in her life.

He'd have liked to ask but she was talking about work again.

'About the IVM?' Fran asked, although what she really wanted to know was more about this man. 'Andy mentioned you wanted someone with experience in taking immature eggs and maturing them in the incubator. Is there some reason you'd consider doing that here?'

He grinned at her, no doubt guessing she was deliberately introducing work into the conversation to keep away from anything personal, but the hint of mischief in his expression did something weird deep inside her.

More than physical attraction?

Surely not!

She concentrated on his answer.

'I know the idea is still very new,' he was saying, a smile still lurking around his lips, 'and it's probably presumptuous of me to want to try it here, but there's a couple who have been through two cycles of IVF and each time the drugs have made the woman quite ill.'

He paused, looking around the deck before he looked back at her.

'I wouldn't have given her the second lot of treatment if she hadn't been insistent.'

'Desperate for a baby?'

Steve nodded.

'So I thought,' he began, breaking into Fran's thoughts of the couple she didn't know, and what they must have suffered, 'that instead of giving her the drugs we take a few immature eggs and raise them in the incubator, then fertilise them when they're ready.'

'That's a fabulous idea,' Fran told him, secretly thrilled at the idea of having total responsibility for nursing the immature eggs to maturity. 'Andy has had a good deal of success with IVM, and I've been involved with the immature eggs. Me and a couple dozen lab assistants and other embryologists.'

But here they'd be *her* babies, those little eggs, and the thought of having sole responsibility for them made her smile at the man who had brought her to this place.

Unfortunately he smiled back and she felt again that tug of something deep inside.

Don't think about it!

'You cooked so I'll clear up,' she said, standing up and collecting the scattered dishes and cutlery from the table, walking to the kitchen, so aware of Steve the nerves in her spine were prickling from his presence behind her.

She rinsed off the plates and tucked them in the dishwasher, wiped down benches, dithering.

Two kisses on the beach didn't mean a thing, really, so why the dithering?

Because she wanted them to mean something—to at least lead somewhere…

She went into the bathroom to wash her hands and freshen up, splashed water on her face and returned to the table outside, where Steve had moved their chairs together so they could look out through the wilderness of bushes to faint glimpses of the sea.

He'd also poured her another glass of wine, and one for himself.

She sank down into the chair and picked up the wine, sipping at it carefully because he was so close, his shoulder all but brushing hers, the closeness causing a slight tremor in her fingers.

She wondered if he'd noticed, because he took the glass from her hand and set it on the table, then turned and licked the wine from her lips, murmuring appreciation—of the taste?

Or of her lips?

'There is no need to hurry this, whatever this might turn out to be,' he whispered. 'In fact, Hallie had a very good rule.'

He pulled Fran onto his knee, his lips against her ear.

'And that was to never make decisions at night.'

'Never make decisions at night?' Fran echoed, looking into the face so close to hers.

'Exactly,' Steve said. 'Sleep on it and if, in the

sober light of day, you still want whatever it was then you know it's okay.'

'Sleep on it?'

Fran knew she was repeating his words like a demented parrot, but her mind was so befuddled she couldn't help it.

'Sleep on it,' he repeated, then he set her on her feet, gave her a pat on the bottom, and pointed her in the direction of her bedroom.

'Now!' he added, in a stern voice. 'Before I stand up and kiss you again and then it will be too late!'

Which left her in no doubt about the decision she had to make...

You're here to work!

The reminder, her first thought on waking, was enough for her to put all thoughts about decisions right out of her head. She ate her breakfast and drank her coffee—alone, as Steve was apparently out somewhere.

Work?

Or absent because he didn't want to discuss

the previous evening and whatever decision she might have reached?

Setting aside the skittering of excitement even thinking about making her decision triggered, she turned her mind resolutely to work and headed to the lab to see how things were going.

As she crossed the courtyard, she was adding up the hours. Mrs Red's eggs had been introduced to Mr Red's sample at about three in the afternoon so now, seventeen hours later, she should be able to tell if any of the eggs had been fertilised.

After sixteen to eighteen hours you could usually tell, so maybe Mr and Mrs Yellow's might be showing some success as well.

Excitement for her work took over her thoughts and she hurried into the lab, pulling out the first of the four red dishes that held Mrs Red's eggs. As she put it beneath the microscope and peered at it, she saw the two tiny bubbles—the pronuclei—in the centre of the egg.

This one was already dividing.

Perfect!

She couldn't help just a little fist pump. Working alone in the lab—Steve had mentioned an assistant but so far he hadn't appeared—she had no one to share her excitement, but that didn't mean she couldn't show it.

Returning the dish to the incubator, she took the next red one.

Damn! Joy never lasted long. There were definitely three bubbles in it, which meant two sperm had penetrated and the egg was unlikely to develop normally.

But dishes three and four were both good. One thing she and Steve had covered in one of their colleague-type conversations over dinner the first evening had been that he was happy to implant two embryos but not three, although implanting two would only be at the request of the client. They had facilities to freeze any extra ones, so that was no problem, but as yet these weren't embryos, not until cell division began.

She tucked the three good dishes back into the incubator and pulled out one of the yellows.

No luck so far, and no luck with any of the

dishes. Still, some eggs took longer to show they'd been fertilised.

The reminder didn't help the uneasy feeling inside Fran's stomach. Sometimes the outer shell of the egg was too tough for the sperm to penetrate and they had to be helped. It was a delicate procedure but she was adept at it, although here— without the necessary equipment?

But they had the eggs—good eggs…

She went in search of Steve, her mind so wholly on the problem at hand—or the suspected problem—that for the first time since she'd met him she didn't feel a start of awareness at his good looks, although her heart did skip a beat when he smiled.

'I know you haven't got a stable table for ICSI but do you have the other equipment? A really good microscope, an ultra-fine pipette, some medium to slow the sperm? I've more of Mr Yellow's sample—'

'Whoa!' He held up his hands to stop her flow of questions. 'Do you always get up and rush straight into work mode no matter how late or long the night was?'

She had to smile.

'Don't know,' she admitted, relaxed in a way she'd never felt before. 'I'm not used to late, long nights. And, anyway, last night was hardly late.'

She thought it best to ignore the part where she had lain awake for hours, wondering what she was letting herself in for...

'But you could get used to them?' he murmured, coming so close the words seemed to wash across her skin.

'I guess,' she said, remembering her earlier decision to be mature about this—to play it as a game, to have fun! 'But to get back to the Yellows?'

He looked so confused she had to explain.

'I call them by their colours. I find it easier than trying to remember names and match names to colours.'

'And if they're just colours you don't have to get personally involved?' Steve queried, amazed at how much he was learning about this woman—

learning and liking. But why would she hide her deep humanity behind her brisk all-business disguise?

'Self-protection?'

'Of a kind,' she admitted, 'not that it always works, as you saw yesterday.'

He touched her lightly on the shoulder.

'Don't hide your true self,' he murmured, then finally answered her original question.

'Yes, we have the necessary equipment for the rather amazing intracytoplasmic sperm injection. How could we consider doing IVM without it? Surprisingly enough, while we don't have a laparoscope, we do have a microscope with micromanipulators. You wouldn't have seen it as it's locked away. The manufacturer donated it when we bought a number of new ones for the lab in Sydney, and arranged for us to get the pipettes and other equipment needed for the clinic here. Do you want to have a go?'

'I thought I could try one egg,' she said. 'You drew five out of Mrs Yellow, so I could do one egg and the others could still be fertilised anyway, but I'd like to try now while Mr Yellow's specimen is still viable.'

'Go for it. I've got the next couple coming in, but Alex is there and I think Arthur, your lab assistant, has finally turned up, so he can stand by for the eggs. What colour next?'

'Green,' Fran said without the slightest hesitation, so definite he had to ask.

'For any particular reason? Do you go in order? Red, yellow, green? Traffic lights?'

She grinned at him and his heart felt as if a giant fist had grabbed it and squeezed hard, jolting him enough that it took a moment for him to catch up with Fran's reply.

'No definite order, and today just seemed to be a green day. I ate breakfast on the back deck and the green of the foliage out there seemed to glow with intensity—not, I suppose, that plants can really glow with the joy of life!'

Steve shook his head, surprised that the uptight professional woman he'd first met should be having such flights of fancy.

He couldn't put it down to a few kisses surely.

Or had she made a decision about where the kisses might lead?

'So, green,' he said, not wanting to reveal just how far his thoughts had strayed, or wanting to analyse why he found himself thinking about her so much.

He led Fran into the lab, introduced her to Arthur, another giant islander, who nodded and smiled, taking Fran's hand so cautiously he might have been handling fragile glass.

'Do you have the key to the special cabinet?' Steve asked Arthur, who nodded again and pulled at a strip of leather that hung around his neck, producing a bunch of keys.

He selected one shiny enough to suggest it was rarely used and unlocked a cupboard Fran had previously not noticed, as, unlike the others, it was flush with the wall.

The new microscope was still wrapped in plastic, its attachments still in their separate compartments in the felt-lined metal case.

'Oh, you little beauty,' Fran breathed, though she was jolted back to reality by Steve's laughter.

'So, you talk to your equipment, too,' he teased, and she turned and smiled at him, suddenly at ease with the situation in which she found herself, at ease with the work ahead of her, and the pleasure she suspected would come from whatever relationship she had with this man, limited though it might be.

Which meant she'd decided to go where the kisses led? a voice in her head asked.

She ignored it and concentrated on work.

'I only talk to equipment when it's top-class, like this one,' she told Steve, wondering if he was thinking about her decision.

Work!

'And if we could get some thick rubber matting—is Akila the best person to ask for that?—we could put it under one of the small tables here in the lab. It would provide some cushioning, although with the concrete floor there's unlikely to be much movement anyway.'

She could feel the excitement of the challenge building inside her, and wondered if it was brimming over—showing in her face or manner.

Arthur was studying her with wide eyes, although that might have been confusion, but Steve was definitely smiling.

Smiling...

Focus, she told herself, although the warmth the smile had transmitted into her body was extremely pleasant.

'We need the microscope with the micromanipulator attachments,' she explained to Arthur, 'because the pipettes we will be using are so fine you can't actually see the tip with the naked eye. I know Steve has a couple to see, and he'll want one of us to get the eggs, but if you go with him—we're using the green pack for them—I'll see Akila and get the microscope set up and then wait until you come back to do the injection.'

Arthur's smile gave her a different flush of warmth and as the two men headed off to the procedure room to deal with Mr and Mrs Green, Fran went in search of Akila to ask about rubber matting.

Like a conjuror producing a rabbit from a hat, Akila returned before Fran had finished unpacking the microscope's attachments and to-gether they set four thick rubber mats on the floor then put the table on top of them, Akila finding weights to hold it firm so the four legs sank into the rubber.

Fran checked the yellow dishes again, but the sperm still hadn't penetrated any of the eggs.

They *could* be slow, she told herself, but years of practice told her that was probably not the case. If Mr and Mrs Yellow wanted a baby, she would have to help fertilise the egg. The good thing was that the percentage of successful fer-tilisations using the pipette was high—sixty to eighty percent—so as long as she didn't muck things up, all would be well.

Arthur returned with Mr Green's specimen, and Fran washed and checked it while she waited for the eggs. Four eggs, they found, when she and Arthur examined the fluid from Mrs Green. Fran asked Arthur to separate them out into the dif-ferent dishes she'd already set up with the media they needed to nourish them.

For all his size, he worked with a delicate precision, so well that Fran congratulated him and won another gleaming smile.

They tucked all the dishes into the incubator and she was wondering whether Steve might want to watch the manipulation of Mrs Yellow's egg when Arthur spoke for practically the first time since they'd met.

'I am very excited to be watching you do this. I have read about it, of course, because I am studying to do more lab work, but I have never seen it done.'

While Arthur retrieved one of Mrs Yellow's eggs and the remainder of Mr Yellow's specimen, Fran unwound the layers of wrapping around the pipette and, searching through the refrigerated cabinet, found the viscous fluid into which she could put the sperm.

'It slows them down,' she explained to Arthur, 'to make it easier to pick up just one of them. The tip of the pipette is sharp enough to penetrate the shell of the egg, and then a little pressure on the top of the pipette and in it goes. The main thing is to make sure you don't go in far enough to damage the nucleus of the egg.'

Forcing herself to concentrate, which meant banishing all wayward thoughts of Steve from her head, Fran went ahead with the delicate procedure, so excited when she succeeded that she moved away from the table to high-five Arthur, who had watched over her shoulder the whole time.

'That is wonderful,' he said, as they continued their mutual congratulations. 'We haven't had the microscope very long and there haven't been any IVF patients for a few months.'

His words intrigued her.

'Don't other doctors come when Steve's not here?' she asked. 'I understood he wasn't the only visiting specialist.'

'Others come but sometimes not for a while. Steve says it's hard to get a regular commitment—the doctors have wives and families, you see, and it isn't always convenient. He's looking now at doctors nearing retirement, or using doctors with young families to come in the summer holidays. Steve comes three times a year. He says it's easy for him, not having a family so no ties to anyone, but he is a kind man and clever, so he should have a family.'

A strange sensation stirred in Fran's stomach. Regret?

Impossible!

If the kisses led to anything, it would be a holiday romance, nothing more. She had known that since he'd first talked to her about his list.

CHAPTER FIVE

APPARENTLY STILL EXCITED at having seen the procedure, Arthur became positively chatty as he washed Mr Green's sperm while Fran separated Mrs Green's eggs into different dishes.

'So, are you ready for my IVM patient?'

Steve's voice made them both turn towards the door.

'She's here? Now?' Fran managed, although the lingering excitement from the ICSI success together with Steve's sudden appearance had sent both her mind and her body into a spin.

Think work!

The reminder wasn't quite enough to stop the bodily excitement, but it did snap her mind back into action.

'Of course,' she said. 'I've made a pack of purple equipment—the colour of royalty for a very special couple.'

Dazzled by the happy smile that accompanied the words, Steve could only stare at her.

Could this be love, this strange new emotion he was feeling?

Of course not! He barely knew the woman, and, yes, he was attracted to her, but *love*?

'Good,' he managed when he realised she obviously needed some reply. Then, encouraged by managing one word, tried a few more. 'Will you collect them for me?'

Another smile, another missed beat in his heart. Ridiculous!

'Of course,' she said. 'I'd love to.'

Love to?

Love?

'Good,' he managed, monosyllabic again—pathetic really! 'Alex is here to man the ultrasound.'

Hoping he hadn't made a complete fool of himself, he headed back to his clients, but an image of Fran as she had flashed that smile persisted in his head.

She was in a bog standard lab coat, with, no doubt, her sensible uniform of shirt and shorts underneath. Her hair was pulled back in the neat scroll affair she'd been wearing when he'd first seen her, *and* it was covered with a lab cap!

Hardly the clothing of an enticing siren!

Yet his body couldn't have reacted more strongly if she'd been stark naked.

He had to get past this, as it was just too distracting.

After the one disastrous relationship he'd had with a colleague—ending in a broken engagement—he'd avoided mixing work and pleasure. In fact, he'd found that he enjoyed getting right away from work when he had leisure time, enjoyed the company of women who had little to no idea of what his job entailed and even less interest in it.

Relaxation.

That's what he'd sought! Companionship, a bit of fun, evenings out and, yes, some healthy sex thrown in...

'So, have you checked on the ultrasound for immature follicles?'

Now her voice made him start, and it was only with considerable effort he suppressed a groan.

'Yes, they're fine. I think I can take two. Though I think that when they mature, you'll have to use ICSI on them.'

She smiled again, this time the happiness shining in her eyes.

'A doddle,' she said. 'Arthur and I have just fertilised one of Mrs Yellow's eggs. The equipment you were given is top-class.'

Which explained her excitement.

And why should that make his spirits flag?

She followed him up to the treatment room, where the Hopoates waited, the powerful mix of tension and excitement vibrating in the air around them.

Once again, he was impressed by how naturally Fran could put people at ease. A few kind words, a smile, a joke, and they were eating out of her hand.

She told him she was using purple colours because it was the colour of royalty.

'But *we* are royal, though you didn't know,' Mr Hopoate said. 'We are from the southern islands, so not royal like your Queen but descended from what would be considered royal in other places. In our island group we are called the Masters of the Heavens and the Masters of the Canoes.'

'Master of Heaven and Canoes, I like that,' Fran said, and Steve could tell her interest was genuine.

'These are our titles from the old times,' Mr Hopoate said. 'That is why it is important to us to have a child. Royal blood should be passed down, even now, because it is important our history and traditions are carried into every generation.'

He was so serious, Steve felt his heart falter. And he, who prided himself on remaining detached, uttered a silent prayer to whatever fates watched over these beautiful islands, a prayer that the Hopoates would be blessed with a child.

'Ready?' Alex said to him, reminding him he was here to work, not rely on prayer.

He nodded.

With IVM, Mr Hopoate's specimen would not be needed until the eggs matured, so his role was just supportive.

And support he did, holding his wife's hand and telling her how much he loved her and how, even if this didn't work and they couldn't have children he would still love her.

Steve glanced up as he was depositing the precious eggs in the purple-marked dish Fran was holding for him and was surprised to see tears in her eyes.

So he wasn't the only one who'd got emotional...

The urge to touch her, comfort her in some way, was strong, but at the same time he wondered if it was more than the sentimentality of Mr Hopoate's words that had upset her.

After all, what did he know of this woman to whom he was becoming increasingly attracted?

Fran took the eggs back to the lab, adding some serum from Mrs Hopoate's blood, which Alex had prepared for her.

'These,' she said to Arthur, 'are extremely precious. This is the first time Steve has taken immature cells so it's up to us to see they're given every chance to mature, after which we'll use ICSI on them, so watch carefully when I do it, so you can do it next time. I'm sure with the skill Alex already has, and your help in the lab, it won't be long before you don't need Steve or any other visiting doctor. You'll have your very own IVF unit and be the envy of all the South Pacific nations!'

'I think that would please Steve,' Arthur said, 'because, although he likes coming here, I think he'd also like to settle down and start a family. I see the way he handles the babies people bring in to show him—babies he's helped create. He is a man who wants babies of his own.'

Fran closed her eyes. Gentle Arthur had no idea of the wounds he'd just dealt her—stab wounds in her chest, her lungs, her heart.

Not that Steve wanting babies was anything to do with her. All they'd done was kiss…

And if the kisses made her burn all over, then that was *her* problem!

* * *

'Mr and Mrs Green brought two small chickens, denuded of feathers, cleaned and even boned,' Steve said when she had finished work, showered, changed, and wandered out onto the deck.

He was standing by the giant barbecue, the luckless birds plastic-wrapped and sitting in a cool box beside him.

'Without the bones they'll squash flat to make it easy to barbecue them. I've just rubbed a few herbs and some lemon and oil over them and left them to marinate for a while. I'll cook them both then there'll be cold chicken for lunch tomorrow.'

Fran studied him, sensing some change in his mood. No, more behaviour…

She'd spent the day with a stomach knotted by anxiety over the decision she had made—to let the kisses lead where they may. And now he was acting as if there'd never been a kiss, let alone the possibility of something to follow it.

He put the chickens on the hot plate and gave them his full attention so all she could see was his back, and what could you glean from a broad, straight back?

'There'll be things for a salad in the refrigerator if you wouldn't mind putting one together to go with these,' he said, throwing the words casually over his shoulder.

Fran left, only too happy to get away from what felt like a particularly tense situation.

Though why?

Steve heard her footsteps retreating to the kitchen and let out a sigh of relief.

He hadn't seen *that* much of her during the day, but when they had been working together it had been as if the kisses of the previous afternoon and evening had never happened.

He should have forgotten Hallie's dictum about decisions made in the evening and taken her to bed when their kisses had prompted it.

Now he had no idea where they stood. Had she thought about it, made a decision? If so, she'd given no indication of it.

Maybe he'd imagined the previous afternoon

and evening—imagined the heat of the kisses they'd shared...

He reached into the small refrigerator and pulled out a light beer, then put it back, deciding he didn't really need it.

Maybe wine with dinner...

Maybe nothing.

Dear heaven, but he was making a mess of this!

And where was Fran?

Surely mixing a bit of lettuce and tomato together couldn't take this long?

He turned the chickens, the aroma of their crispy skin making his mouth water.

Then, suddenly, she was beside him, close but not touching. Close enough for every nerve in his body to be aware of her.

'Salad's on the table and I ducked back to the lab to check on our purple eggs. It's too early to say but they seem to be maturing happily.'

'Happily?' he echoed, turning to her so he caught her smile, and her lips were right there, and everything was all right.

'Must rescue the chickens,' he muttered against

her lips when they'd been kissing with a desperation he'd never felt before.

She drew away, half smiling though there was a faint frown line between her eyebrows and a bemused look in her eyes.

He lifted the chickens onto a platter and followed her towards the table, where she'd not only left the salad but had scattered flowers, as he had done the night before.

He selected the most perfect of the hibiscus and held it in front of her.

'Which ear?' he asked, and her smile improved.

'I suppose left on a temporary basis,' she murmured.

'A temporary basis?'

The smile had faded, and the faint frown line had reappeared.

'It's all it can be, Steve,' she said firmly. 'A holiday romance, a little fling. It's this place and its magic that's drawn us together. To try and make it more back in the real world would spoil, probably destroy, something wonderful.'

Well, at least she thought their 'fling' would be wonderful.

But why the proviso?

They were two adults—mature adults, even—who were attracted to each other. Why should it not continue when they returned to Sydney?

But something in her demeanour told him not to query it so he slid the vivid flower into her hair, settling it behind her ear, wanting to draw her close, to hold her, but aware they'd miss their dinner if they kissed again.

He served her a tender chicken breast, and they ate, and talked of work, of family, and the meal done, the debris cleared away, they relaxed. He told her of Liane, the damaged foster sister he'd adored, who'd turned to him again and again when she'd lost her way, but somehow he had failed to save her.

Fran reached out and took his hand, drawing him towards her.

'You can't save someone who doesn't want to be saved,' she said quietly, adding, 'And you shouldn't break yourself trying to fix someone else's problems.'

Maybe someone should have told him that a long time ago, for he'd very nearly broken himself. He *had* lost his fiancée, and for a while very nearly given in to the despair of failure.

Had his face given him away? It was the last thought he had as she leaned across and kissed him.

A gentle kiss, empathetic and yet redeeming. A kiss that grew to something else…to need and want and passion.

Standing now, his hand against her head, beneath the soft brown hair, holding her close.

Kissing her because now he had her answer.

Fran found herself responding, kissing him in turn, slowly and carefully, relishing the contact of nothing more than lips until his hand slid from beneath her hair and his fingers trailed down her neck to slide a button undone and delve under the fabric of the opening, sliding beneath her bra to take the weight of one breast in his hand.

Her body stiffened, wanting more, uncertain

how to ask until a small whimper whispered from her lips. He caught her breath in his mouth and increased the pressure of his fingers, finding her hardened nipple, teasing it, while his lips still held hers captive.

She wasn't going to whimper again—whimpering was needy—but she did gasp as his fingers nipped her sharply, gasped and shifted against him as desire, hot and demanding, speared down to the moist place between her legs.

'Bedroom?'

He breathed the word as lightly into her mouth as she'd whimpered her need earlier, but didn't wait for a reply. Instead, turning, he hooked an arm around her neck to keep her close as they walked back into the house.

And the kisses didn't stop, on her temple, on her ear, little kisses, barely brushing her skin, yet so erotic she was trembling again.

His bedroom—she was pleased about that—the bit of her still capable of thought decided.

But once inside there was no hurried rush of shedding clothes, no ripping or tearing. He was slow, teasingly slow, achingly slow, yet she was happy to let him set the pace.

Steve let his hands explore her, wanting to know her shape, aware in some dim recess of his mind that her hands, too, were on a voyage of discovery. His shirt was definitely unbuttoned, and he had the sensation of a feather brushing across his chest, across his nipples, pressing them lightly.

But most of his concentration was on Fran, on the silky texture of her skin, on the kisses he was trailing along her jaw line and down her neck, touching the pulse before moving on to taste the perfumed honey of that shadowed skin between her breasts.

Now, clothes a puddle on the floor, shoes and underwear in tangled heaps, the urgency to feel skin on skin so great there was no more thought.

Relief as skin met skin. Relief and relaxation as bodies fitted to each other, soft to hard, warmth transferring, parts matching as nature had intended, pleasure in the sharing of touch

and feeling until excitement built again and demanded more.

Steve tipped her back onto the bed and lay beside her, exploring again, his eyes holding hers,
trying to read her reactions to his touch in her
shadowed eyes. They gave away little, although
he saw colour flare in her cheeks as he thumbed
a nipple, enough colour to prompt further ex-
ploration, holding one full breast while he took
that nipple in his mouth and suckled hard on it,
feeling Francesca's body arch, her hands reach
out for him. But he kept on teasing, wanting to
be certain that she wanted him as much as he
wanted her.

Teasing, touching, kissing, until she whispered,
voice husky with desire, 'Steve, I need you!'

It was more than an invitation, more than a
plea, and he slid into her welcoming heat and
prayed he wouldn't come too soon, desperately
thinking of the seven times table to distract himself. But not even seven times nine could distract
him from the joy of Francesca's body, or the way
she moved beneath him, uttering little cries of

pleasure or delight, arching up to him, her arms clasped around his back, fingernails dragging through his skin as if she needed more and more of him inside her.

Her legs clamped him now and they moved as one, riding a tidal wave, a tsunami of such power it swept them onto some distant, explosive planet, finally beaching them on a very foreign shore.

'My God!'

The words escaped Steve's lips as he lay exhausted on the no longer smooth bedcover.

'I couldn't have put it better myself,' Francesca muttered, but then she laughed, lying on her back and laughing, the sound so joyous Steve had to smile. Touched by it in some way, he took her hand and held it, while he too joined the laughter.

Was laughter a normal reaction to good sex?

He couldn't remember laughing after sex before tonight, but actually, if he was honest, what he'd just experienced hadn't been good sex, it had been mind-blowing, cataclysmic, all-consuming, out-of-this-world sex.

And why had they laughed? It had seemed natural at the time, but now he thought about it…

'You're wondering about the laughter,' she guessed. She'd propped herself on one arm and was looking down at him, still smiling, while the forefinger of her right hand traced the contours of his face. Slick with sweat, her skin was silvered by the moonlight that lit the room, and the tumble of hair that had escaped captivity was a dark cloud that partly hid her face.

She was beautiful, so beautiful.

'Probably totally inappropriate,' she admitted, 'but, oh, Steve, that felt so good! It was as if I'd never really made love with anyone before—never known it should be fun! So surely there's nothing wrong with enjoying it while we can?'

She sounded just unsure enough for him to reach up and pull her down on top of him so he could kiss her as he reassured her that there was definitely nothing wrong with it.

Fran let him kiss her, her mind far too busy to be concentrating on kissing him back.

For a start there was her reaction to what had

just happened. Shouldn't her body be burning with shame and confusion and probably regret?

Why should it?

She was a free agent, she could have affairs with anyone she liked—not that she ever had or probably ever would again, but there was nothing to stop her, was there?

'Are you regretting it?' Steve asked, no doubt alerted to the fact he'd lost her by her lack of response to his kisses.

'No way,' she told him.

'Good,' he said, nipping teasingly at her lower lip, then sucking on it, sending her nerves into a new frenzy. 'Because it was something special between us and shouldn't be regretted.'

'Mutual attraction—I'd heard of it, of course, but never really known what it was,' she murmured, but although her mind was managing the conversation, her body was squirming on top of his, moving to ease the need that was building again...

She shifted to the side, propping herself up

again while she studied his face, or what she could see of it in the gloom.

A lazy smile drifted onto his lips, and his dark eyes gleamed.

Devilishly!

Lying there on the bed, nonchalantly naked, his eyes scanning her face, asking silent questions, he was so beautiful he took her breath away. Not classic-marble-statue beautiful, but man-beautiful. A forceful face, hewn rather than sculpted, slashes of cheekbones beneath deep-set eyes— dark as night those eyes beneath ink-black brows.

Full, sensual lips, pale-rimmed to emphasise their shapeliness, lips that even now were moving, the smile changing from lazy to lustful, tempting her, teasing her, challenging her to make the first move this time.

Or was she imagining that?

'Well?'

The throatily spoken word was definitely a challenge, but could she take charge, make love to him?

The idea excited her, but that was possibly because she'd lost her mind.

'Too late,' he murmured, reaching out to trace a circle around her breast, spiralling it closer and closer to her nipple while her body tensed and tightened, so wound up by the time he touched the pink bud she groaned out loud and flung herself into his arms, pressing her breasts against his chest to stop further torture, yet knowing she wanted more, needed more.

Slower this time, learning from each other, learning what pleased and excited—delaying the final act and satisfaction because the foreplay was such fun.

She was on top of him again, looking down into his face, and she saw the gleam in his eyes and the slight smile on his lips as she made her admission.

'Really?' he asked, touching her again, still teasing, but his fingers brushing her skin so deliberately delicately that she wanted to yell at him to press harder. Which he eventually did, before spinning her into orbit somewhere in outer space, into a world of dazzling lights and sparkling fires that shook her body to the core.

And this time when she collapsed on him, she was pleased he'd shouted out her name right at the end. She fell into an exhausted sleep, waking, confused about where she was, at two in the morning with a man she barely knew sound asleep beside her.

His arm lay heavily across her waist and as she tried to ease out from under him, he murmured a protest and turned to pull her back, tucking her into his body so he surrounded her.

Oh, the bliss of it! To be spooned so safely against a man. Nigel had never held her like this, neither had he liked to feel her wrapped around him, although as a child she'd always thought that must be the nice part of a marriage…

Not that this was anything to do with marriage, or even a future—that was impossible—it was a holiday romance, nothing more!

Fun sex, that's all it had been, and all it would be.

But thinking back—remembering—embarrassment crept in.

Embarrassment?

There had to be a better word—a stronger word—for how she felt right now. Embarrassment at her lack of restraint, at the laughter, at the things she'd said...

Steve wouldn't be embarrassed, so neither should she be. She should be mature—heaven knew, she was that—and sensible about this relationship.

Enjoy it, definitely, and remember it with pleasure, but keep her emotions in check so at the end she could put it behind her as easily as he would.

She snuggled closer, knowing this wonderful safe haven wouldn't last and that she had to make the most of it, glean memories from it to keep her warm in the future.

Memories to ease the ache she suspected she would feel in her heart?

CHAPTER SIX

HE WAS GONE when she woke—in his bed—and confusion over what to do next fluttered like moths in her head.

Should she muss up the bed in her room?

Of course not, she'd made her own bed every morning she'd been here. Why was she even thinking this way?

To stop thinking about facing Steve in daylight?

That moth was bigger than the rest, and its sudden presence got her out of bed, gathering her clothes and fleeing into her own room, where she crawled into bed for comfort rather than deception.

But there was work to be done, and she was being pathetic.

Pulling the sheet over her head, she hid from the truth.

The truth that she had truly enjoyed their sexual encounter?

Where was restraint in that?

She thought about that restraint, the one that had shaped her thoughts and her decisions since childhood.

Because of the guilt she'd felt when her father had left them, certain for some peculiar childish reason it had been her fault? Because she'd trodden so carefully after that, perhaps subconsciously not wanting to lose her mother as well?

Nonsense! That was the past—gone so long ago it should be forgotten.

She was a mature woman and although, admittedly, she hadn't considered it post-divorce, she was entitled to a love life. She bounded out and headed for the shower. Those moths were not going to spoil her memories of a wondrous night.

She was eating breakfast when Zoe arrived.

'Steve still out on his run?' she asked, a question that explained why he wasn't around in the morning.

'Must be,' Fran replied, hoping she sounded more together than she felt.

But there was work to be done and she'd need her wits about her, so work!

Steve appeared, freshly showered, as she was walking to the lab.

'Good morning, lovely lady,' he said, with a smile that warmed her all over. 'Can we check the red dishes? And the green ones? Forty-eight hours and we should be seeing some cell division on the reds and it's probably late enough to see the pronuclei in the greens.'

Fran smiled at the enthusiasm in his voice, though she did wonder if he was feeling all the physical things she was feeling.

Like wanting to reach out and touch him, to move closer.

Work!

She couldn't deny that Steve was passionate about his work but…

Then he did touch her, one finger tilting her chin so their eyes met.

'Okay?' he asked, and she knew her smile in reply was probably way too delighted but she couldn't help it.

'Very okay,' she told him. 'So, come with me while I check?'

Years of experience at ignoring any emotional highs or lows—mostly lows—made it easy to switch into work mode, although every nerve in her body was aware of Steve's presence, and it took a great deal of strength to not accidentally brush against him.

Arthur was already in the lab and as he lifted the dishes from the incubator she slid them under the microscope, checking each one before stepping back so first Steve and then Arthur could see the progress.

'Look, this one is nearly perfect,' she said, excited in spite of herself as she studied one of the Reds' embryos. 'I know the fact that they divide evenly isn't really an indication of their strength or viability but the even ones always appear stronger to me. Far better than the ones that are lopsided or are dividing too quickly. That first one we checked had divided unevenly.'

Memories of the night of love fled now as she was caught up in the miracle of procreation, although she continued to be sure she didn't stand too close to Steve.

The next two were also good, and they moved on to the green dishes, where pronuclei were visible in two of them.

'It's early yet,' Fran reminded the two men. 'Give them time.'

'So, now you will look at Miss or Mister Yellow?' Arthur asked, when he'd returned all the checked dishes to the incubator, clearly keen to see their success with the ICSI.

Fran smiled at him, his enthusiasm was so infectious.

'Let's check the other yellows first, to see if they've been inseminated without help.'

Nothing had happened, although one egg had divided without insemination, which was a common enough occurrence. It would have to be let go.

'Okay,' Fran finally said to Arthur. 'Now we'll check the last one, the one we helped.'

He carried the dish carefully over to the microscope and Fran, not wanting to look, waved her hand.

'You check it first,' she said, and Arthur bent obediently over the microscope, adjusting the eyepiece then lifting his head to beam at them. 'See for yourselves!' he told them.

They did, followed by high fives all round.

The Blues were the first couple to arrive that morning, Fran holding the dish with its special bath of fluid as Steve collected the eggs. Fran talked quietly and comfortingly to the couple all the time, ignoring the man doing the procedure as much as possible.

Wanting to separate out the eggs herself—and perhaps because her restraint was wearing thin—she sent Arthur in for the Browns, then, as the little polar body appeared on each egg, she divided Mr Blue's specimen, washed and cleared of impurities, between the dishes and tucked them away, understanding now why such a small set-up had such a large incubator.

She checked the purple eggs, smiling as she realised they were maturing nicely. Knowing he'd be trying IVM for the purple couple, Steve had made sure they had the chemicals and growth hormones ready for them and Fran had carefully fed the eggs the nutrients they needed.

Thinking that tomorrow they'd be ready for the ICSI, she realised that she'd have to speak to Steve about collecting Mr Hopoate's specimen.

Maybe now?

No, concentrate on work. She must check to see if Mr Yellow's specimen still had viable sperm and if so, let Arthur do the ICSI, or at least the first stage of it, which involved clearing the little cloud from around the egg.

But as she squinted into their regular microscope and saw that the only moving sperm were very lacklustre, Fran realised that they would need a new specimen before they could do the ICSI.

Checking the remaining yellow eggs, she found them fine, nourished in their special liquid, so it seemed a shame not to use them.

Now she had *two* valid reasons to see Steve.

Pathetic, that's what she was, but at least it *was* a relevant work visit.

Arthur hadn't returned with the Browns' samples so she went up to the clinic, meeting Arthur on his way back to the lab.

'You can get on with separating the eggs and cleaning the specimen. I won't be long, I just want to see Steve about a couple of things.'

She could have left off after the 'I just want to see Steve' bit and it would have been true.

And *really* pathetic!

Steve's smile as she walked in produced what were, by now, familiar sensations of tingling, slight breathlessness and a warmth in her belly.

He introduced her to the Browns, who had a complicated Vanuatuan name she knew she'd never pronounce, let alone remember. It was good to meet them in spite of Steve's contention that she thought of them by their colours so as not to get too emotionally involved.

Alex was also there and, after assuring Fran he'd contact both Mr Yellow and Mr Purple, he walked out with Mr and Mrs Brown, giving Steve the opportunity he'd been waiting for since he'd seen Fran earlier this morning.

Even as she explained her mission, he'd drawn her close, holding her against his body until she finished with a faint '…so we need another specimen from Mr Yellow.'

'Got the message—messages,' he murmured, her lips so close to his she could have breathed in the words.

Then he kissed her, slowly at first, enjoying the taste of her once again, feeling a heady intoxication as she kissed him back.

Her fingers slid into his hair, while his hands roved her back, remembering…

'We're at work,' she reminded him softly when they'd drawn apart in order to breathe.

'Don't I know it,' he groaned, then he kissed her again, hard and fast.

'Later,' he said, releasing her and sending her on her way with a last touch to her cheek.

'I've a meeting at the hospital so won't be here for lunch, but when you finish for the day, we could go north to Havannah? There's a resort there and the most beautiful beach. We can swim, laze about, maybe have dinner in the restaurant.'

Stay the night?

It was off season, so the resort would have rooms.

No, best not push things, but he knew she would love the place and the thought of seeing her in a swimsuit, swimming with her, had already produced a frisson of excitement in his body.

And maybe, before they left, in the week while they waited for pregnancy tests, they could go to Kukuhla, the most magical little island in the group and only a short boat ride from their island of Efate.

But as he walked across to the hospital he wondered about her proviso—her insistence that this would be no more than a holiday romance, a fling.

The obvious answer was that she was seeing someone back in Sydney, which, given she was a clever, bright, attractive woman, was highly likely.

But it didn't fit with what he knew of her, or thought he knew of her.

She was too open, too honest to cheat on a significant other...

Although the little she'd shared of her private life—married and divorced—told him he really didn't know her well enough to judge.

So why did he feel he did?

No, he didn't know, and considering his own failed romance, maybe he was just a bad judge of women.

No, and no, and no! He couldn't believe she'd be cheating on another man...

Havannah Beach was everything a tropical beach should be, Fran decided when Steve pulled in, not to the resort but just above it, almost onto the sand itself.

She dug in her bag for suntan lotion, and was

smoothing it on her arms when Steve took it from her.

'Hop out and I'll do it. You'll never reach your back to cover it properly.'

She did as she was told but was reluctant to remove the sarong she'd wrapped around her bikini—the sarong Steve had given her on her second night in Vanuatu.

But the decision was taken out of her hands.

'I've been wanting to do this since I first gave it to you,' Steve told her, undoing the knot that held the material together, and unwinding it from around her body.

'Ah, just as I thought—perfection!'

Her hands wanted to move to cover what for her was nakedness, but she struggled against the familiar need for restraint.

'You haven't done a lot of swimming in that bikini,' he teased, squeezing lotion into one hand. 'It'll be cold when it goes on, you know.'

And with that he proceeded to give her the most sensual experience she'd ever had.

No, remembering the previous night, she had to

amend that—the most sensual experience she'd ever had with clothes on.

His hand, slick with lotion, slid across her skin, while sexual tension slithered along her nerves, tightening them almost to breaking point, even when he turned his attentions to her back, his hands straying ever so slightly now and then.

'You're done,' he finally announced, his husky voice suggesting she wasn't the only one who'd been affected by the process. 'Let's swim!'

He took her hand and led her down the beach, white powdery sand sinking beneath her feet. The water was a pure, translucent, blue-green colour so even when she'd walked in up to her thighs she could still clearly see her toes.

Steve dived in and swam then dived again, coming up right in front of her, his skin bronzed and beautiful, water droplets that she had to touch gleaming on chest and flying through the air as he flicked his hair.

'Coward!' he challenged, and she took the plunge, diving down to touch the sand then swimming out into the blueness of the deeper water.

Swimming back, he met and matched her stroke for stroke until their bodies touched and all restraint was broken.

They twined together in the water, bodies touching, lips searching for skin to kiss, and then for lips.

'We'll drown,' Fran whispered to him as they drifted into deeper water.

'As if I'd let harm come to you,' he said, and looked deep into her eyes, so she couldn't miss the message that he meant it.

Her heart somersaulted and she wondered just how foolish her decision to have this little romance had been.

Already she suspected it was more than attraction on her part, but if Steve felt that way—no, it was too complicated. Just live for now and enjoy it—don't think about the future.

She kissed him, although moths were once again fluttering in her head. He wasn't a man who *didn't* think about the future...

He lifted her, still kissing, so she lay in his arms

in the water, and the moths disappeared, flooded out by passionate sensation.

The sun was sinking before they left the water and dried themselves, Steve pulling on his shorts and shirt before rewrapping her, slowly and teasingly, in the sarong.

'We'll walk up to the resort and have a drink as the sun sets, then dinner so we don't have to waste time with that when we get back.'

'Waste time?' she teased, so thoroughly relaxed a new Fran seemed to have taken over her body. A Fran who teased, and kissed in public, and ached to get back into bed with this man she barely knew...

This time she woke early, Steve still in bed beside her. She lay there thinking how wonderful their lovemaking had been—lacking the wildness of the previous night but still exhilarating.

He stirred and pulled her tight against him, then groaned.

'No doubt you know what I'd *like* to do,' he murmured in her ear, 'but if I don't run one morning it's easier to not run the next, and it's running that keeps me sane in this work where we have such disappointments as well as successes.'

She turned in his arms.

'Can I run with you? I run at home, but mainly because I love the rush it gives me.'

His arms tightened.

'Put some clothes on and we'll run together.'

But as she pulled on a pair of shorts and T-shirt, Fran wondered if this was a good idea.

If too much togetherness was a bad thing. Wouldn't it bring them closer? It was the one thing she really didn't want because the closer they became—out of bed—the harder it would be to leave him.

Not that running left them with breath for conversation, although sharing a love for a morning run seemed to make them more of a couple, which—she reminded herself—was what they couldn't be. He had his list, and on that list was his desire for a family. With children.

But running with him along the top of the ridge behind the town, and through a little forest path he seemed to know well, was so exhilarating she forgot her doubts and just enjoyed the view out over the island-studded ocean, and the darkness and smell of the rainforest when they took the little path.

She knew he was matching his pace to hers, which was slower than usual after a week or so of not running. Firstly because she'd been so busy before she'd left it had been one thing she couldn't fit in, then after the flight and settling in over here, although she'd brought her gear, it hadn't occurred to her.

Other things on her mind?

She knew that brought a foolish smile to her face and was glad she'd dropped a little behind him so he couldn't see it.

They ended up beneath the clinic and had the hill climb at the end, so Fran arrived back in their temporary home and collapsed into the nearest chair.

'I thought you were a runner,' Steve teased, and she glowered at him because he was barely out of breath.

'It was the hill,' she retorted. 'You finished with a hill!'

"That's the bit that gets the endorphins surging,' he told her. 'But while you sit there, recovering, I'll have a quick shower and duck over to the hospital. I usually have breakfast over there with Alex while we map out a timetable for the next specialist visit.'

'Which is usually you?' Fran asked, and he nodded, dropped a quick kiss on her hair and disappeared towards his bedroom.

He was such a *good* man, she thought as she watched him go, she had to hope he didn't feel too much for her—that he had accepted the temporary nature of their relationship. And given his goals, how could it *not* be temporary?

He'd been hurt before, she'd known that when he'd spoken of the sister he couldn't save. The pain she'd seen in his eyes had made her want to hold him and keep him safe from pain for ever.

But nobody could offer that...

Steve showered then left, reluctantly, for the hospital. He'd far rather have been having breakfast with Fran. He found himself hoping he hadn't pushed her too far on the run, knowing she hadn't run since she'd arrived.

Yet running with her had been special. Another bond between them.

Which brought him back to thinking about her insistence that their relationship would end when they left the island.

Not that thinking about it did much good. He barely knew her, so how could he possibly work out what she was thinking?

And hadn't he, himself, decided that work and relationships didn't mix?

Forget it, Fran was different!

Wasn't she?

Returning to the clinic after breakfast, he went straight to the lab. Today was the day! The red eggs would certainly be ready for transfer—one to Mrs Red's uterus, the other to be frozen for future use, and he guessed the yellow that Fran had inseminated would also have reached sufficient development for transfer.

Fran was at the lab when he arrived after breakfast. Why wasn't he surprised? One thing he did know about her was that she loved the work she did, and was excited by the progress of her tiny eggs.

'Will you transfer today?' she asked as he walked in.

He grinned at her.

'I've got both the Reds and the Yellows coming in, although why I've picked up your use of colours for their names I do not know! I've always been quite content to use the clients' names and now you've got me calling them by colours.'

'Not to their faces, I hope,' she said, and he smiled again because *she* was smiling and a smiling Fran did something to his insides.

'And Mr Hopoate—royal purple and the Lord of Heavens and Canoes—is he coming in to give a specimen?'

'This afternoon,' he told her, then firmly turned his attention to work, making arrangements for the transfer, checking the Yellow egg Fran had fertilised then deciding not to transfer it until the next day.

'But you'll get him to leave a specimen so we can fertilise the other viable eggs?' she asked, and he nodded.

'All under control,' he assured her. 'See you at ten.'

He left the lab, aware he could have lingered there all day. The woman had definitely got under his skin.

And again the question nagged of why the limitation. On that first night when he'd held the flower to put behind her ear, she'd said right, which meant there was no man in her life.

So?

Whether it was a night of slow and languid love-making, or the run, Fran wasn't sure, but the desire to be near Steve, close to him again, was so overwhelming she went up to the clinic rooms far earlier than she needed, to find not only the Reds already there but another couple she didn't know.

And a baby!

Not quite freshly minted but fairly young, and Steve was holding it in his arms and talking to it, making the infant smile and gurgle, its shiny dark skin almost glowing with delight at the attentions of the man who held him.

And there's your proof if you needed any, Fran told herself, that there's no future for you with this man. Forget the list, he's obviously made to be a father and probably, from the look on his face, longs to be one.

The pain of this confirmation was so strong she felt her knees weaken and had to lean against the desk for a moment to recover her equilibrium.

You love him, the voice in her head continued in accusing tones, and she knew it was correct.

So, learn to live with it.

Steve was introducing her to Mr and Mrs Tamou.

'Mrs Tamou and Mrs Inui are sisters. It was Mrs Tamou's success that prompted Mr and Mrs Inui to come to us.'

He was smiling at her over the baby and she felt her heart break, but fortunately part of her brain was working and it understood he was telling her the names so she wouldn't call Mr and Mrs Inui Mr and Mrs Red.

She shook hands all round, admired the baby, who was being handed back to its mother, then thankfully the Tamous departed.

Steve was practically glowing.

'A lot of the couples come back with their babies,' he told her, sure she'd share his delight. 'It's the best part of this job.'

'I'm sure it is,' she managed to reply.

'But that's not why you're here, is it?' he said, his smile still so bright it hurt. 'Let's get on with things.'

He led the Inuis into the procedure room, explaining what he was going to do. He would give Mrs Inui a light sedative, although this part was painless, then he'd transfer the little embryo to her uterus.

'It can float around in there for up to a week before it settles into the uterine lining,' he told the excited couple.

Or sometimes doesn't settle in, Fran thought as

painful memories of failures added to the pain she was already feeling.

But she kept a smile pasted on her face as she left the room, not wanting to intrude on the couple's exciting moment. Mrs Inui would rest in the treatment room for a couple of hours, and although she could resume normal activities afterwards Fran knew from experience she'd probably take it easy, not wanting to dislodge the tiny seed.

She was checking the purple eggs when Steve came in.

'I've got the Yellows coming in later,' he said, 'and although I'll wait another twenty-four hours before I implant, do you still want a new specimen from Mr Yellow?'

'I think so,' she said. 'The eggs are still viable and look strong and if we manually inseminate them and they produce embryos we can freeze them, which would save Mrs Yellow going through all the early IVF processes. We can just monitor her and implant another one when she's ready.'

He shook his head.

'You're assuming this first one won't implant,' he chided. 'Be positive! I know the percentages of failure as well as you do, but we have to always believe we'll have success, otherwise what's the use?'

Fran had to turn away so that he wouldn't see her pain.

If she had believed during that third time, might it have been successful?

Probably not! Not according to her doctor, who had been lamenting her lack of eggs and predicting early menopause.

Steve watched her turn away, but not before he'd seen the shadow of what looked like pain in her lovely eyes.

Had she gone through IVF unsuccessfully herself? Was that why she was so attuned to their clients?

Was that why her marriage had broken down?

He longed to ask her, but she was bustling around the lab, now taking out one of the purple dishes to check the egg development.

He could almost feel the defensive barrier she'd erected around herself.

With him on the outside...

Work! he reminded himself. *You, too, can be professional...*

'Will it—or they—be ready if we get Mr Hopoate's specimen this afternoon?' he asked.

'I'm pretty sure they will be.'

No smile!

'Here, look for yourself.'

She stepped away from the microscope. A step longer than necessary?

So as not to brush against him?

Or him against her?

Steve didn't have a clue what it was, but he knew that in the time between when they'd finished their run and now something had shifted in their relationship.

They'd hardly spoken except about work and then in the presence of other people, so it couldn't be something he'd done or said.

Had she received a phone call from home? A text, or an email?

Could he ask?

'That looks good,' he said, realising she was probably waiting for a response.

He straightened up and reached out to touch her on the shoulder.

'You okay?' he said quietly, and was surprised to see tears well in her eyes, though she blinked them back with a fierceness that told him he wasn't meant to see them.

'Fine,' she said, but he knew it was a lie.

She was busying herself with the other purple dishes now, looking at them with naked eyes before shifting one to the microscope.

'I have to go back to the Inuis,' he said, 'but I'm not going to the hospital, so perhaps we can have lunch together.'

He supposed it was a statement that didn't need a reply, so after a brief pause he went back to the clinic.

Something was eluding him and he had no idea what. In truth, they'd known each other barely a week, so he could hardly expect to fully understand her—if such a thing was ever possible between two people.

But he tried anyway, thinking back to the fairly uptight woman he'd met off the plane, then seeing the gradual change in her as the island worked its magic. In bed, he'd discovered, she was a woman who held nothing back, and yet she was obviously holding back a whole lot of who she was.

His thoughts were becoming so entangled he forced his mind away from Fran, turning it to the couple he was about to send home full of hope and probably a little apprehension.

They were standing with Alex in the waiting room as he explained when they should come back, giving them a date in nine days' time.

'We'll do the pregnancy test then and again at twelve days to be sure, and we want you to be positive about this. Yes, we've talked about the statistics and you know it might not happen with your first IVF cycle, but remember that it can and possibly will, so hold tight to that thought.'

Alex was good, Steve thought. Maybe in another year he could head up a permanent IVF clinic here. He, Steve, could afford to sponsor another O and G specialist for the hospital and the two could work together as he and Alex had.

And then he could get on with the last item on his list because he wouldn't have to leave a wife and family for four weeks three times a year.

Was he thinking that because he'd met Fran?

Liked Fran?

Maybe loved her?

Had that thought somehow flown through the air and transmitted itself to Fran, causing her to ask, as they were finishing their lunch, why, with a family so important on his 'to-do' list, he hadn't started earlier.

'I did think about it,' he admitted, then knew he wanted her to know.

'I did more than think about it. I met a woman, got engaged, made plans for a wedding in the not-too-distant future, and children. I'd finished my intern year and residency and was starting my O and G specialty so I was well on my way.'

He paused, mainly because the memory still hurt.

'Then Liane turned up. The stepsister I told you about. She'd always considered my apartment as a second home. You have to understand that Liane had been badly abused as a young child. She was a broken spirit, and not even all the love Hallie and Pop gave her could fix her. But she was special and we all loved and protected her.'

'Such a terrible thing for a child,' Fran said quietly, obviously understanding, so Steve continued.

'She was on drugs at the time, and as low as I'd ever seen her, so I spent a lot of time with her, helping her reduce her intake gradually so that she didn't suffer seizures. Finally, I got her into a detox centre. She came out so well and happy that I thought if she got away for a real holiday, this time the detox might work.'

'And how was your fiancée with all this?'

Fran asked, although no doubt she'd guessed the answer.

He studied her, thinking back to that time.

'I'd always thought she understood—understood that to me Liane was family, so I had to take care of her. It didn't make me love Sally any less, and I thought she knew that.'

'Did you tell her?'

He paused, startled by Fran's words.

'She'd have *known*,' he said. 'Although I knew, at first, she was slightly put out that Liane needed so much of my attention, I was sure she understood. But it was only when I paid for a trip to Bali for Liane that Sally got particularly frosty, reminding me I'd been promising she and I would have a holiday like that. We worked through it somehow but when Liane returned, she was determined to start afresh and focus on her career. She was a wonderful singer. It wasn't long before she hooked up with an agent who offered her a flat, a job and, eventually, drugs.'

'Poor woman,' Fran said, shaking her head.

'Poor woman indeed,' he said, remembering the

woman he'd loved for so long when she'd come back to his place that last time. 'She turned to me again when she discovered she was five months pregnant by someone she'd met in Bali—and although she wanted the baby and knew the drugs were bad for it, she couldn't keep off them.'

He'd been toying with his fork but now he looked up at Fran.

'I had to take her in, but it was too late. The baby, Nikki, was drug addicted when she was born, and Liane died soon after.'

'And your fiancée?'

'Gone the day Liane came back that last time. Gone because she felt I cared more for Liane than I did for her.'

'She was your sister,' Fran said, reaching out to remove the fork from his hand and hold it in hers.

'She was. And when I was ten years old I had loved Liane. But Sally was to be my wife! I should have seen what was happening, understood how she felt, made more of an effort to help her accept the situation.'

'And would that have helped?' Fran asked.

He shrugged and shook his head, the memories so painful there were no words.

Although…

He took a deep breath.

'Actually, apart from losing not only a fiancée and also a good nurse, and *not* marrying at that stage of my life, the rest of it turned out all right. One of my other foster sisters adopted Liane's baby, and battled through the early years when little Nikki was so sick. But in the end, by sheer serendipity, she met and fell in love with Nikki's birth father—the man Liane had met in Bali. They're married now and expecting another child, so fairy-tales do happen.'

'Just not to you?'

He looked up into Fran's lovely eyes.

'I was beginning to think perhaps they did,' he said softly, and saw tears well again as she shook her head, let go his hand, and began to busily clear the table.

But talking of the past—of Sally—had reminded him that relationships with work colleagues weren't a particularly good thing.

Although Fran was only a temporary work colleague...

CHAPTER SEVEN

WHILE THE NIGHTS remained filled with sensual delight and sexual satisfaction, the days developed a routine, Steve implanting tiny embryos, Fran freezing those that had developed sufficiently to be used in the future. It was here that she had to be meticulous, showing Arthur how to choose the best ones to freeze, then how to extract all the water from the tiny bunch of cells, replacing it with a special anti-freeze.

Next came freezing, placing the tiny embryo in a straw, cooling them very slowly so no shards of ice formed to pierce the precious cells. Once frozen, the straws went into canes, and with this the embryologist had to be particularly careful with identification. Fran continued using coloured tags within the little containers, further labelling them all with names and numbers corresponding to the various couples.

But even though she was busy with the freezing, she was finding the wait for confirmation of pregnancy very difficult. She knew it was partly because it brought back memories of her own days of waiting, but it seemed worse because she knew and liked these people, had spoken to them, and now dreaded to think how they'd react if they found the IVF cycle they'd been through had failed.

'Worrying about failure?' Steve asked, breezing into the lab where she had been watching Arthur do ICSI on Mrs Yellow's eggs.

'Do I look worried?' she snapped, mostly because seeing him unexpectedly like this did terrible things to her heart, and different terrible things to her body.

Her heart was weeping because it knew their time together was nearly over, while her body still wanted to rush him off to bed—or anywhere private—every time she saw him.

'Yes,' he said, coming closer and resting his

hand on her forearm. 'Knowing the statistics—that terrible forty percent success rate that's considered the norm—we're all entitled to worry. But we never take on patients unless they've been through a lot of counselling and they know the odds as well as we do.'

'I know, I know,' Fran said. 'I suppose it's different because I've met them, talked to them. Back in the lab at the hospital in Sydney, I not only didn't know the couples, but often I didn't know who'd conceived and who hadn't. This is too close, I suppose.'

Steve was watching her as she spoke, and guessed there was more to it than she said. She was as uptight as the couples who were waiting for news, possibly more so. And in bed there seemed to be a desperation in her lovemaking, as if she wanted to drown out all thought with passion.

Could he take her away?

Over to Kakuhla?

He did the numbers in his head.

'What's worrying *you*?'

Fran's voice broke into his calculations.

Aware Alex was in the room with them, he had to phrase his reply carefully.

'I was thinking, as we're nearing the end of your visit to the islands, I could show you around a little, maybe take you over to Kakuhla Island, which is beautiful and not too far to travel.'

'But won't the Reds be ready for testing about the same time you're implanting the embryo in the Purples?'

He nodded. He might have known she could add up as well as he could.

'I was thinking that I could leave Alex to do the first of the pregnancy testing—after all, the couples involved have no doubt been doing tests themselves. But then I realised I couldn't— couldn't let down the couples by not being there should this cycle have been a failure. I want to be the one with them, and to talk to them about options. It's why we stay a month.'

He brooded on it for a moment, then rather reluctantly added, 'Although you could go over to the island, or do a few island-hopping trips yourself. Zoe would be happy to show you around.'

Her smile was so bright he was struck by the realisation he loved this woman, so when she said, 'You're a good man, Steve Ransome,' he was filled with happiness.

And knew he had to fight to keep her.

He left the lab, needing to think through this latest development.

Yes, he'd known almost from the start that he'd wanted the relationship to continue when they both returned to Sydney because she was intelligent, good company, understood his work and another dozen reasons, including their compatibility in bed.

But love?

He'd set romance aside after the disaster with Sally. Instead, he'd concentrated on learning all he could about IVF before setting up his own clinic. There'd been women since, but none had been more important than his work, so they'd shared mutual enjoyment and passed on.

But Fran was different.

Fran really was a keeper!

But how to convince her that they were meant to be together?

Did she not love him?

That was certainly a possibility but their love-making was no longer 'fling' stuff, it had grown into something special, wild at times admittedly but nurturing, caring...

Loving?

He shook his head, going back into the clinic to talk to Alex because thinking about Fran was driving him insane.

Especially when she appeared five minutes later, not having given him time to get her right out of his head.

'What about the other couple?' she asked. 'The ones you said might not be quite ready for egg retrieval. Surely by now they would be?'

Still reeling from the realisation that he was in love with her, Steve couldn't work out an answer, so Alex took the question.

'The cycle failed,' he said quietly, and Steve saw Fran flinch. 'The eggs failed to develop. Steve and I were discussing it now, thinking we might try IVM on them. Not right away, of course, because the cycle might have caused some special problem, but in a couple of months.'

Fran nodded, although the pain she felt for this couple was almost overwhelming. Her third cycle had ended this way, and that's when she had been told it would be useless to try again.

Which had seemed only to please Nigel.

She turned to Steve. 'You'd come back to do it?'

'Alex and I were talking about that as well. I've got a young O and G specialist who's been working in my clinic for a few months. I'm wondering whether, with his experience and Alex's, and a good embryologist, they could do it themselves. It's where we'd always hoped to go, to have people here who could handle the whole process.'

Fran thought about it for a moment.

'Do the islands have the population numbers to make it viable?' she asked, and he smiled.

She wished he wouldn't—it distracted her—so she had to catch up with what he was saying.

'Probably not, although time will tell. But it wouldn't have to make a profit and the hospital can use the services of two O and G specialists. The embryologist would be a problem as there wouldn't be full-time work.'

And suddenly a way opened up and the future became clear.

Steve was setting this up so he could be at home, finding a wife, starting a family, so…

And Andy would know…

Talk to her about it…

Which would be a thousand times worse than her mother's progress reports on Clarissa's pregnancy, which, now she came to think of it, no longer bothered her at all!

'I could stay,' she said, letting the thought settle about her and feeling how right it was. 'I don't need a full-time income, and I already love this place and the people. I could help with counselling too, because I've done that with couples who want to know how the whole process works. I'd have to give notice at work, and sort out my apartment, sell or rent, pack up, but I could do it.'

'That would be wonderful,' Alex said, 'because your job is so important to the whole cycle. Arthur is good but he is still learning, and with your experience you could help with advice to me, and the new doctor, should we need it. We could make a wonderful team.'

'Andy would kill me for taking you away from him,' Steve said, although his voice seemed strained as if there were other things he'd rather be saying. 'He went on about it enough when I only wanted to borrow you for four weeks.'

'Andy has plenty of good people to take my place,' she told him. 'I should know, I trained most of them.'

'Then maybe one of them might like the island life as much as you seem to,' he said, and she had to smile, although she knew it was a weak effort.

'I was here first,' she said firmly, although inside she was quaking, well aware she'd made this decision because it seemed to solve her loving-Steve dilemma. Removed from him by a large ocean, she'd surely get over him one day?

'Well, if you're really serious that's a fantastic

offer,' Steve said bluntly, 'but I think we're running before we can walk. Alex and I were still at the talking-about-it stage, and I'll be back in three or four months anyway so the couple who failed can join that programme. Now, if we're quite finished here, I've got an appointment at the hospital.'

Alex looked rather surprised by this announcement, and as Steve walked out the door, Alex turned to Fran.

'What's eating him?' he asked. 'I've known Steve for years and although I've seen him upset when cycles don't produce pregnancies, and angry when people make mistakes, today he just seems grumpy, and I'd have sworn he was one man who didn't do grumpy.'

'Everyone does grumpy,' Fran told Alex, hoping she didn't sound similarly bad-tempered.

She left the clinic, going back down to the quarters, feeling thwarted. For a few minutes it had seemed as if she'd been offered a lifeline—a way of getting away from Steve for long enough to get over him—but he'd cut it off.

Although…

She remembered Andy asking her if she'd known Steve, way back when this trip had first been mooted, and she'd told him no, so if they'd both been living in the same city for years and hadn't run into each other, how likely was it that they would when they got back?

Unless he persisted with this idea that whatever they had could continue in Sydney.

She should tell him.

And have him pity her?

Hadn't she had enough of that from Nigel's colleagues' wives, who had apparently known about her trouble getting pregnant from the start?

Former friends they were now, unable to understand the pain she felt whenever she saw their happy, healthy, children.

Body in automatic mode, she'd pulled food from the refrigerator while these dismal thoughts raced through her head. But looking at it now, the makings of a salad, a wrap to put around it— she didn't feel hungry. She had nothing to do, so she'd go for a walk—maybe even a run.

* * *

Steve made his way over to the hospital, only too aware there was no reason for him to be going there, although he knew he'd find someone to talk to or something to do.

Not that he'd be much use to anyone, his mind was too full of questions.

First was the revelation that had struck him back at the clinic—the realisation that what he felt for Fran might be love.

Could it be?

His reaction to her offer to stay on here certainly suggested it was. He'd felt physically sick at the thought of not seeing her, not sitting with her over meals, sleeping in the same bed.

His gut was still knotted, while his brain was circling helplessly around her offer.

She wanted to stay *here*?

Because she'd grown to love the place?

Hardly! She seen two beaches, a restaurant and barely knew the place at all.

Or could it be a way of escape—either from something happening back at home or from him?

She was adamant that their relationship must end when they left the island, so maybe offering to stay on was her way of making sure that it did.

That made the most sense, but wasn't it a bit drastic? Shifting countries to avoid a relationship?

What of her friends and family?

He was sure she'd mentioned a mother.

It was at this stage he realised just how little he knew about the woman he loved.

There, the word had come out with no hesitation that time, so maybe it *was* love.

He had to find out, get to know her better, which seemed ridiculous given they'd spent almost every night since she'd arrived together.

He turned and headed back to the little apartment they shared. They'd go to lunch down at the waterfront—there was a lovely seafood restaurant just out of the main town.

But she wasn't there.

Fran had walked down through town, listening to the sounds of this strange, exotic place, revelling in the aromas of food and flowers and sea.

She *could* live here.

Her mother would have a fit at the very idea, but eventually she'd give in and come to visit. After all, these days she loved to travel.

Her mother would meet the local people, realise how special they were, see the beauty of the beaches, and...be convinced it was why her daughter had chosen to live here?

Fran shook her head at the thought.

It wouldn't have to be for ever. Steve would soon find another woman—there'd be plenty of women who'd love to marry him.

Not that he'd mentioned marriage, but where else would continuing this affair lead?

Regret for what could not be seized her, clutching at her stomach, burning in her lungs.

She wouldn't cry, she'd used up her life's allotment of tears years ago.

Realising she'd reached the waterfront, she wandered along to a small café, went in and bought a sandwich, and a pretty fruit drink that tasted more of coconut than anything else she could name. Then she sat on the jetty to have lunch, seagulls swooping in circles above her, waiting for her to drop a crumb.

Looking out over the clear waters of the bay calmed her mind and body to the extent that she realised that, yes, she could live here. Maybe not for ever, but certainly for a year or two…

Though walking back up the hill in the heat of early afternoon made her think maybe not.

Silly really, even considering it all, when there was no certainty that Steve would go ahead with his plan to have a permanent IVF clinic here.

Silly, too, to think he'd pursue her back in Sydney. He was a rational, intelligent man and no doubt once back in the real world he'd totally forget her. She was making mountains out of molehills, as her mother would have said.

'You do realise why we're both a bit tetchy,' Steve greeted her when she finally reached their accommodation and sank down in the shade of the deck.

He was standing leaning back on the railing, the green jungle growth of the garden behind him. 'It's because tomorrow's the first testing day. Reds, and the day after that the Yellows. We mightn't be consciously thinking about it but those doubts are there, nibbling away at the edges of our minds.'

He flung out his hands as if to say, *There, what do you think of that?* and Fran had to smile.

In fact, she realised now she *usually* had to smile when she saw him, even when he was causing chaos in her body.

'Anyway,' he continued, 'we've done no sightseeing lately.' A wicked grin flashed across his face as he winked and added, 'Can't think why not!'

For someone who didn't blush she wasn't doing too badly at it since she'd come to Vanuatu. Fran just hoped he hadn't noticed, and waited for what was coming.

'So, this afternoon I'm taking you to the Blue Hole. Swimming costume and shoes that can get wet are the order of the day. The rocks around the water are mostly coral and very rough. It's fairly shaded but suntan lotion is a good idea. I'm happy to help with that.'

He came towards her as he finished speaking, took her hands and pulled her to her feet, looking deep into her eyes, his eyes saying things she didn't want to hear.

His arms enfolded her, holding her close, and when she finally relaxed into his arms, she leant against him and longed for this to be her place.

Eventually he moved, easing her away from his body so he could look into her face again.

'Okay?' he asked, and she nodded, then headed for her bedroom to get dressed for their outing.

It wasn't okay, Steve knew, as he too headed for his room to get organised. Her eyes had been shuttered against him, her thoughts and feelings hidden behind a blue-green wall.

At least the Blue Hole was magical enough to bring a smile to her face, her expressions of delight so genuine his heart began to hope again.

'It's actually a series of pools, the last of them opening to the ocean down that narrow end. You can't see it for the jungle but it means the water is a mix of salt and fresh.

She pulled off her shirt, revealing the pale body he was beginning to know so well, and handed him the sun lotion as if it was the most natural thing in the world.

He smoothed it onto her skin, making sure he covered all of it, wanting to protect her now, thoughts of sex far from his mind.

'I think I can manage the front,' she said, smiling at him as she turned and took the bottle from his hands.

Had his hands lingered too long on her smooth, straight back? On the swell of her hips, the narrowness of her waist, the delicate bones of her spine?

He'd been learning her in a different way, although he knew full well he didn't know her. Not in important ways! Didn't know much about her past—married and divorced, full stop—or what brought the shadows to her eyes, or what kept her from committing to him when they were back in Sydney.

She finished putting on the lotion and handed him the bottle.

'For all you've got to-die-for olive skin, you should put some on your face.'

And although he knew the fierce heat was gone from the sun, he did it because she'd suggested it.

'Last in's a wuss,' she said, diving neatly into the clear water.

He followed and came up beside her, pleased there were no tourist ships in port and that it was a weekday so they had the pool to themselves.

'Like it?' he asked, and was rewarded with a brilliant smile.

'Love it!' she said. 'It's the rainforest crowding all around it that make it special. And the jungle vines there, like the ones Tarzan swung on, so you can imagine him and Jane splashing around in here.'

She paused then added, 'Though if you do a "me Tarzan, you Jane" joke I'll probably hit you.'

It had been on the tip of his tongue but, duly warned, he shut his mouth, diving down to find one of the smooth pebbles that lay among the rougher coral rocks on the bottom of the hole.

He brought one up, pleased it was a pretty one, and handed it to her.

'A present?' she said. 'But it's lovely!'

Then somehow they were kissing, and soon doing more than kissing, their coming together almost cataclysmic in its intensity, so when he held her afterwards he knew his trembling was matching hers.

'We must be cold,' she said, with a pathetic attempt at a smile.

'We must be,' he agreed, then stopped further conversation with a long, deep and very satisfying kiss.

Fran eased away and swam, up and down the small part of the pool Steve had chosen, her mind in chaos.

She loved this man and was reasonably sure he might feel the same way about her, but how could she deny him the family he had wanted since he'd been ten years old?

She couldn't, and that was that.

Neither could she tell him about her failed attempts at IVF. He was such a positive man, there was never a glass half-empty for him. He'd want her to try again, urge her to, but the last failed attempt had almost broken her, and she knew, for certain, another one would do the same.

And then he'd walk away?

She couldn't blame him, knowing how important children were to him, but she'd had enough men walk away from her, with her father and then Nigel, and she knew just how much it hurt...

But if it succeeded?

Hope flared but common sense reminded her that what Steve wanted—needed—was a family, not another only child.

And she loved him too much to deny him that.

He was swimming beside her now, matching his strokes to hers.

Perfectly!

She stopped, feeling for the bottom, feeling also the pebble he'd given her pressed against her flesh in the bikini top.

And when he stopped, it was her turn to reach

for him, to hold him in a close embrace and kiss him.

She had just one more week of kisses and she intended making the most of them.

CHAPTER EIGHT

OR DID SHE?

Steve had obviously decided not to wake her for a run so she woke in his bed—alone.

And remembered it was the first pregnancy testing day—the Reds.

The Inuis. She knew them, knew their names, had sat with them while Steve had extracted Mrs Inui's eggs.

And knew also they had a less than fifty percent chance of being pregnant.

She burrowed under the sheet, an ostrich hiding its head from the world.

But Steve expected her to be there for the test, wanted her to share the excitement.

Except it might not be excitement.

She clenched her teeth to stop a wail of fear and pain escaping from her lips then reminded herself she was a mature professional woman and this was just part of her job.

She didn't believe the words she told herself, but it was sufficient to get her out of bed, into the shower, then dressed for work.

Shirt and shorts—so prim and so boring!

So unlike the woman she'd become in three short weeks...

She poured some cereal for breakfast, added milk, then tipped it out, her stomach refusing to accept that she should eat.

This was idiotic, she had to positive!

It had worked for Mrs Inui's sister—there was a beautiful baby to prove it—and how many of the women she'd met at the clinic when she'd been going through IVF had produced babies?

Most of them.

Eventually...

She made for the bathroom, cleaned her teeth and tied up her hair, tucked the stone Steve had given her inside her trouser pocket, then with heavy steps and an even heavier heart she headed up to the lab. She'd check the purple dishes first.

But the thought of them made her close her eyes. If she had the power to ensure just one of their couples tested pregnant, it would be the Hopoates so their reign as Lords of Heaven and Canoes could continue.

Steve appeared as she was showing Arthur the healthy little embryo Steve would implant later in the day, and she wondered if the power of positive thinking would help this little group of cells grow into a royal heir or heiress.

Steve's appearance broke into her silent conversation with the dish so she slid it back into the incubator and, with already taut nerves tightening more, turned to look at him.

'Ready?' he asked, the smile on his face as radiant as the sun.

She stared at him. He *had* to have felt for the setbacks as his clients—the same disappointments when pregnancies failed—yet here he was, so positive she almost began to believe herself.

Hiding her turmoil of feelings, she agreed that she was ready and, leaving Arthur to man the lab, walked with the man she loved up to the clinic.

The Reds—Inuis—were already there, and from the lack of smiles on their faces and the droop to their shoulders Fran knew they'd used a test kit from a chemist to find out for themselves.

But Steve, though he must be used to seeing couples come in like this, refused to lose his cheerful smile, greeting them heartily and explaining that home tests weren't always accurate.

These days they are, Fran thought, but she didn't share it.

Alex handed Mrs Inui a small specimen jar and she dutifully retired, bringing it back and handing it to Steve.

He asked them both to sit down, then took the jar into the consulting room.

'I know I could test it in front of them but I feel this gives them more certainty,' he said to Fran, who had followed him in.

Or allows a little more time for hope to build again so they'd be twice disappointed, she thought, but didn't say, although her heart was sinking lower every moment.

When the test came back negative, all of her hopes disappeared to ash, leaving a bitter taste in her mouth and an ache in her heart.

But she said all the right words when Steve talked to the Inuis, explaining how they could proceed after this, testing again in three days' time just to be sure.

Then he spoke of the alternatives if the later test didn't prove positive and this cycle didn't produce a pregnancy. Fran even joined in, telling them stories of friends who'd become pregnant on the second or third cycle of the treatment, giving them hope *she* hoped was realistic.

But after they left, Fran returned to the lab, asking Arthur if he would take the Purple embryo up to the rooms when the couple arrived.

'I know I should be there,' she said to him, 'but I feel a bit deflated and thought I'd walk it off.'

After warning her that it was really too hot to be walking, he let her be, so Fran was free to slip down to her room.

And pack!

In a state of cold numbness she phoned the airline office and accepted a seat on the late afternoon flight, then ordered a taxi to collect her mid-afternoon.

Steve would be busy then with the Hopoates.

The Hopoates!

She had their second embryo to freeze.

Arthur, she was sure, could do it, but somehow these people had become special to her and she wanted to be sure it was safely stored for them.

She hurried back up to the lab, aware that her behaviour was cowardly, but it was self-preservation more than anything else. Her heart just couldn't handle any more hurt.

She pulled out the purple dish and put it under the microscope, concentrating on the delicate task of preparing the precious embryo for freezing, thinking of the couple who might need it if the first one didn't fix itself to the uterine wall.

The pain that clutched her heart at *that* thought told her she was doing the right thing.

She knew these people, *and* she knew the pain of failure.

To go through that with them?

She just couldn't do it.

'Arthur told me you were going for a walk.'

She closed her eyes briefly at the sound of Steve's voice, finished what she was doing, then looked up at him, aware she owed him the truth.

'I'm sorry, Steve, really, really sorry, but I've just realised I can't stay for the rest of the pregnancy testing. I know that sounds pathetic, and I don't know how to explain it, but I just can't. I'm booked on the afternoon flight.'

He stepped towards her, reaching out to lift her unresisting hands in his, looking deep into her eyes, knowing they were welling with tears.

The eyes she loved were puzzled, a frown creasing his brow.

Would he guess?

Had she given herself away earlier?

She couldn't tell. She only knew that she couldn't put into words what she'd been through— not to Steve, maybe not to anyone.

* * *

'You've been through it yourself?' he asked gently, and she sighed.

Of course he'd guess, but the words wouldn't come.

'Tell me,' he insisted, and she managed a nod.

'Twice, three times?'

She nodded again, the lump in her throat too big for words.

'Oh, Francesca!'

He pulled her to her feet and gathered her into his arms, holding her against his body, so close she had to battle the feeling that this was where she belonged.

For ever.

Except it wasn't!

Couldn't be!

She eased away, tried for sensible, controlled, practical.

'I've got to finish this,' she said, returning to the microscope so she could manipulate the embryo into the straw.

But she couldn't get away from him so easily.

He followed her over and rested his hand on her shoulder as she worked.

'Is this your reason for insisting this was just an affair? Because you feel you can't have children?'

Her back had stiffened at his touch but she had to bluff her way through.

'Not entirely,' she assured him. 'I know it might sound stupid, but I've got used to being single. I love my work, I've got friends when I need company, I've made a different kind of life.'

She finished what she was doing and stood up, forcing him to step back.

'It's all I want,' she said firmly, while what she really wanted to say was that, after her father and Nigel, she really didn't want another man walking away from her.

Disappointed in her.

Especially this man—it would break her heart.

Walking away from him, well, that was hurting already—more painful than anything she'd ever experienced—but it was a different hurt.

Steve was studying her as if trying to read her thoughts, but she was surprised by his question.

'Would it have saved your marriage? Was that your reason for going through IVF?'

She slid the straw she'd been working on into the cane, checked the labelling and put it into the unit that would slowly take it down to the required temperature for storage. The machine did this automatically so, having set the final temperature, there was nothing more for her to do.

Except consider Steve's question, which had startled her, only now making her realise it was something she hadn't considered.

She looked into his eyes and swallowed the lump, answering honestly.

'I kept telling myself it would, but in truth I doubt it, and probably I knew it even as I put myself through those endless cycles and weeks of hope, then dashing disappointments.'

She thought about it now. Yes, she and Nigel might have stayed married, but what would have been the point?

Steve reached out and took hold of her hands again, turning her to face him.

'Tell me,' he said, and she shrugged her shoulders.

'Thinking about it now, bringing a child into my and Nigel's marriage would have been a mistake. Yes, *I* wanted a child, longed for a child, ached for a child, but looking back I know I was being selfish. A child would have made *my* life complete.'

She looked at Steve, looked deep into those dark eyes that saw too much.

'I suppose it would have filled the gap that Nigel's playing around had caused in my life.'

She gave a huff of laughter.

'How's that for a reason to have a child?'

Steve drew her close, held her, then kissed her gently on the forehead.

'Go, if you feel you have to,' he said quietly. 'I understand now. But can I call you when I get back?'

She tightened her grip on him—holding him one last time.

'No, Steve,' she said quietly. 'You know it was only ever going to be for here.'

'Because you can't have children? There's more to a marriage than children. More to life than family.'

She kissed him then, just lightly on the lips.

'You know full well you don't believe that, not for a moment.'

Another kiss.

And now she moved more forcefully away, kissed him a quick goodbye, and hurried back to her bedroom, his offer of a lift to the airport floating in the air behind her.

'You've got an appointment,' she called back, all business, 'and I've ordered a taxi.'

Steve made his way back up to the clinic, his mind in a turmoil. But trying to sort out his thoughts was impossible, mainly because what he felt most strongly was anger. It was happening again, a woman he loved walking away from him.

Loved?

That thought brought him up short.

Yes, loved…

And suddenly it seemed as if his whole life had been a series of losing loved ones—his parents, Sally, Liane, and now Fran.

Nonsense, his practical self muttered. People lost loved ones every day, and what's more he detested self-pity.

But this loss felt different, his whole body seeming to be affected by Fran's imminent departure.

Not that he had time to brood, or analyse it.

He'd see the Hopoates and think about it later.

CHAPTER NINE

'YOU'RE NOT SUPPOSED to be back yet,' Andy said, coming upon Fran in the lab three days after she'd returned.

She'd actually spoken to him on her first day back, answering a question about a patient's frozen embryos, but it obviously hadn't clicked with him then that she'd been away.

'Did everything work out all right?' he was asking anxiously. 'You got on well with Steve? Got the job done?'

Fran had to smile at her absent-minded but still very caring employer.

'Got the job done,' she said, ignoring his other questions, though the pain in her heart reminded her just how well she'd got on with Steve. 'I'm back a little early because I wasn't needed for that last week of pregnancy testing.'

He nodded and touched her briefly on the arm, saying more about his understanding with that touch than a hundred words would have said.

'Well, good to have you back anyway,' he said. 'I want to take some immature eggs from a woman who's coming in this afternoon and I really would rather trust them to you than to one of the others, good though they might be.'

'Well, I'm here and happy to look after them,' she told him, and won a warm smile.

'I'm glad you're back too,' Mike, her second in command said when Andy had wandered off. 'I know what to do and how to do it, but the one lot of IVM eggs I've looked after while you were away didn't look nearly as healthy as the ones you've cared for.'

He smiled at her.

'Must be the woman's touch, you make a more natural clucky hen.'

The description took her right back to Vanuatu and the Hopoates, and for all she didn't want to hear about the failures of the couples she'd met, she did hope that the Lords of the Heavens and Canoes had success.

She realised that her face must have revealed her thoughts when Mike asked, 'You're back there, aren't you? Back in the islands? You liked it?'

She smiled, remembering the sheer joy of waking up in that tropical paradise, the beauty, the lush plant growth—Steve—then shook her head.

'Not liked but loved it,' she admitted. 'The place, the people, the beauty—there was a lot to love.'

'Yet you came back early?'

'Not you, too,' she said. 'I've just had Andy on about that. I wasn't needed, okay?'

The snap in her words had Mike shrugging and holding up his hands in an 'I surrender' gesture.

'I only asked,' he muttered as he walked away.

Fran sighed.

She'd told herself that once she'd settled back into work everything would be okay. Her three weeks in the islands would be locked away in a deep compartment of her mind, the door only to be opened now and then so she could relive the happy memories.

But that door wouldn't be opened for a while.

Not until the rawness of leaving Steve had healed and she could remember all the good parts without pain.

Would that day ever come?

'Fran?'

She looked up to see one of the juniors standing in front of her, a specimen dish in her hand. She'd obviously asked a question.

'Sorry, miles away,' she said. 'What was it you wanted?'

So it was back to work and no more dwelling on the past. She'd managed to get through three failed IVF cycles, Clarissa and a divorce, by concentrating on work. She'd get through this as well.

Only getting through this was harder, she realised a couple of weeks later, when the sight of a hibiscus flower on a bush near her apartment sent pain coiling through her body again.

It was because she wasn't feeling well that it was so hard, she told herself. Give it time...

A week later she was wondering just how much time she'd have to give it. And how could she get over it, when every day the rebellious part of her brain reminded her of how long Steve would have been back in Australia, even suggesting she check up on where he lived and driving by there.

No way—that was just too pathetic!

Could he have called?

She'd told him not to...

It was the weather, still miserable and rainy, and her feeling a bit off. Could lovesickness really exist?

Whatever it was, it stayed with her, until ten days later she sat in the bathroom at her apartment, staring in disbelief at the positive pregnancy test in her hand.

'Honestly!' she said at her image in the mirror. 'Call yourself a scientist! How could you not have thought of this earlier?'

Because of all the failures, came the whispered answer.

Or because her gynaecologist had told her quite bluntly, after the third cycle had failed to produce viable eggs, that she had only a few of her life's allotment of eggs left in her ovaries and would probably go through early menopause as a result.

But that was the end of rational thought for quite some time, as her brain whirled with ifs and buts and maybes, delighted excitement mixing with doubt and dread.

Not to mention confusion...

To tell or not to tell was the really big one.

Normally it would be a no-brainer. A man deserved to know he'd be a father, that he'd have a child.

But with Steve?

Steve, who didn't want just one child, he wanted a family—lots of children—well, more than one anyway.

Not that one child couldn't be a family, but not for Steve, not for someone with parents who had so wanted a sibling for him they'd been killed in the endeavour.

If she told him, he would insist they marry and for all the surge of heat that thought generated in her body, *and* the hippity-hoppity bounds of joy in the totally unrealistic bit of her brain, marrying Steve would not be a good thing.

This one pregnancy was probably a fluke— so unlikely she'd never given contraception a thought, though she vaguely remembered in the heat of passion that first night Steve asking and her assuring him it was safe.

Because it always had been in the past.

And apart from the fact that she'd be denying him the large family he wanted, marrying her for the sake of the baby was hardly a good basis for a marriage. What would happen if she lost the baby? Or even if the baby lived but their marriage lacked love?

Would he walk away from her, as her father and Nigel had done?

She made a cup of tea then tipped it out because it tasted awful. Everything tasted awful! She'd have to tell him.

Or leave Sydney?

That was a better idea…

Get a job somewhere else—Perth maybe, or in the UK. Her skills would always be needed. Overseas would be better, less likely that Andy would find out, because Andy and Steve were friends…

The glass of water tasted awful but she drank it anyway, then began to occupy her mind with things other than Steve and telling or not telling. Determined to treat this in a purely practical manner, she sat down and wrote a shopping list of healthy foods, lots of fruit and vegetables and meat for iron, although she could supplement that.

Which was when the sheer miraculousness of what had happened struck her and she laughed with joy and hugged herself and forgot about all the unanswerable questions and went shopping.

Steve had told himself he would wait at least a month after he got home before he would even consider phoning Fran, but the days dragged by so slowly it was beginning to feel like a year since he'd seen her.

He'd thought of a dozen excuses he could use to call in at her hospital's IVF clinic, and had discarded all of them.

He'd lifted the phone to call Andy to assure himself she was all right, and put the receiver down again.

At work, by forcing himself to concentrate on his clients and the huge step they were taking, he could forget for a while. Then someone would say something and he'd be back in the lab at Vanuatu, Fran in shorts and lab coat, her lovely hair hidden by an incredibly ugly cap, and his heart would miss a beat then gallop to catch up and he'd have to breathe slowly and deeply to banish the picture from his mind.

But at home, particularly now with the bloody hibiscus bushes planted by his great-grandfather flowering with gay abandon in his garden, it was impossible not to think about her.

He had to see her—had to talk to her—at least find out if she was all right.

But why wouldn't she be?

He'd begun to hate his sensible self.

So he concocted a plan, phoning Andy for her address, explaining that she'd left before the staff could give her a farewell gift, a thank-you for her help. He told Andy that he'd post it to her.

Steve had half expected Andy to suggest he send it to the hospital, in which case he'd just have to visit the place and try to talk to her in front of colleagues.

But Andy had surprised him, not only handing over the address but also by suggesting that he might like to deliver it in person. Andy was sure Fran would be pleased to see him.

Steve turned the idea over in his head. He wasn't so sure about the pleased to see him part—but, hang it all, what could she do?

Or what could her boyfriend do if he opened the door to Steve?

No, she didn't have a boyfriend, of that Steve was certain. She'd given herself too openly and fully to have been cheating on someone.

And the staff *had* given him a present for her,

a frangipani lei with 'Come back to Vanuatu' written on the tag, and a pretty sarong that would complement her eyes.

He drove to the address, pleased to find she lived in a small apartment block so he didn't have to press a bell and announce his presence to get into the building.

She could have checked the monitor and chosen not answer her door.

He found a parking space for the car two doors away and walked back, apprehension so tight in his chest he had to force himself to breathe.

Then, there she was, bent over the boot of a small red car in the carport beneath the building, pulling shopping bags out and resting them on the ground while she got the others.

'Bought the shop out?' he asked, coming up beside her and bending to pick up six of the bags, three in each hand.

She turned and looked at him, and he watched the blood drain from her face.

He dropped the shopping bags in time to catch

her, although she recovered almost immediately and pushed away from him.

'What are you doing here, frightening the life out of me?' she demanded, blue-green eyes spitting fire.

'I brought a gift from the staff,' he muttered, bending to capture oranges that were rolling from one of the dropped bags.

'Then you can leave it here and go,' she said, and though she probably wanted to sound firm he heard the slight wobble in her voice.

'I'll carry these things up to your apartment first,' he said—no wobble in *his* firmness.

She didn't answer, instead collecting the last two bags and closing the boot, locking the car with a key fob and stomping away towards the steps that led into the old Art Deco building, then up the inner steps, and up, and up, and up.

'You were going to carry all of this up yourself?' he asked, stopping on the second floor landing to catch his breath.

'I do it every week,' she snapped. 'And for

someone who runs every day, you're not doing too well on the climb.'

She'd reached the top floor and was unlocking the door when he caught up.

'You can just leave them at the door,' she said, busying herself hanging up the keys to avoid looking at him.

'I'll bring them in,' Steve told her, aware she wanted nothing more than for him to go. But being here, with her again, seeing her, even from behind, had filled him with such happiness he couldn't walk away.

He walked into the apartment and although he'd guessed from the address that she'd have a view towards the harbour, he was surprised to find he could pick out his house from her windows.

Not that he'd mention it right now.

Neither would he mention seeing the sarong he'd given her thrown over the sofa or the pebble from the Blue Hole on the window ledge.

He put the bags on the kitchen bench alongside the ones she'd carried up, then reached out and caught her hand.

'Can we not just meet as friends, if only this once?' he asked, although every cell in his being was scoffing at the idea they might just be 'friends'.

She looked at him then, studying his face as if she'd never seen it before—or maybe trying to read what lay behind his words.

'I don't think so,' she said quietly, then she removed her hand from his and began to unpack the bags.

She hadn't told him to leave so he didn't, instead watching her unpack the first bag, and then, intrigued, he began peering into the others.

'Have you turned vegetarian?' he asked, registering they contained only fruit and vegetables.

'I only shop once a week,' came the reply, which didn't answer the question or explain the extent of the fruit and vegetable shopping.

Deciding it was too hard to carry on a conversation with someone whose head was stuck in the refrigerator as she disposed of the shopping, he looked around and saw the list she must have been working off—items neatly crossed off.

Of course neatly—this was Fran!

Oranges, apples, celery, tomatoes, on and on until right at the end an item not crossed off—an item not available at the markets or greengrocer.

Iron supplement.

And suddenly the shopping and the sudden faint and her avoidance of his eyes made sense.

'You're pregnant!' he said, waving the list in her face when she stood to get more produce to stack away. 'And just when were you going to tell me?'

Fran could feel the anger coming off him in waves, and suddenly the answer to her 'will I, won't I' questions became clear.

'I was still deciding but I think probably I wasn't going to tell you,' she answered honestly, because she couldn't lie to Steve.

'You weren't going to tell me? And just how was that going to play out? You'd swear Andy to secrecy? Have everyone in the relatively small world of IVF know except the father?'

He had every right to be angry, but she, too, had rights.

'I'm going away,' she said. 'No one will know. Especially not Andy.'

'Especially not Andy because he would tell me?' Steve roared, and Fran took a step back, although she knew full well he wouldn't—couldn't—harm her.

Her or anyone else…

But his being so angry made it all easier somehow.

And now he knew, well, she didn't have to consider the problem of telling him.

Or not!

He was stalking around her living room now, muttering to himself, obviously trying to calm down before he spoke again.

Please let him not be nice to me, she asked any of the fates who might be listening.

It didn't work, for here he was, standing across the bench from her, not touching her, although every fibre of her being was so aware of him they might as well have been touching.

'Fran, I shouldn't have yelled, but can you please explain why, when you knew how much

I wanted children, you were going to keep this child to yourself?'

He was holding himself together with difficulty, she could see that, but although she knew it would upset him all over again, she had to answer.

She looked into his lovely eyes and answered honestly.

'You want children, Steve, plural, not a one-off fluke of a child. If I'd told you, you'd have insisted on marrying me, and knowing my medical history you'd be stuck with the one thing you didn't want, which was another only child.'

She reached out now, wanting—no, needing—to touch him, and rested her hand on his where it lay on the bench.

'I couldn't do that to you, couldn't ruin the goal you've strived for all your life. It's all hypothetical now, I may not even carry this child to term. Just let me be, Steve. I said right from the start it would be nothing more than a short affair, a holiday romance. I *said* it couldn't last. So go and get on with your own life. Find the woman to have your family with, the woman to be mother to your children.'

Steve shook his head.

This was madness!

But she was right, he had to go now—had to get away so he could think about things, think clearly, something he was incapable of doing with Fran standing there, still pale but so beautiful his heart ached for what he'd lost.

Although, he thought as he walked back down the endless steps, she was right in saying she'd told him all along it wouldn't last, so how could he lose something he'd never had?

How the hell could she compartmentalise so well that those three weeks were already filed away under 'holiday romance' in her brain?

Well, she wouldn't be able to do that in the future, with his child there to remind her every day.

His child!

Rage roared through him again but he couldn't let it take control. He had to think, logically and sensibly, about how to handle this.

She couldn't—and she undoubtedly knew it—

keep him from seeing his child and having input into the child's life.

Oh, hell! He didn't have a clue how to think about this, not even where to begin. All he did know was that having input into the child's life was a long way down the track.

And would never be enough.

He walked back to his car and drove home— home to the big house that had so called out for children that his parents had flown to the US for advanced IVF so he could have a sibling.

And had died before they'd got there.

As Steve disappeared out the door, Fran sank down on the floor and buried her face in her hands.

Steve was upset, and with reason!

If only she'd had time to think things through— *more* time.

Right now she was such a jumble of emotions there was no way she could think straight.

Although the one thing she did know was that

she'd upset Steve—hurt him badly with her flippant 'wasn't going to tell you' remark.

That would have cut deep.

She shouldn't have said it, shouldn't have pretended she'd already made the decision.

Unable to think, she closed her eyes and hugged her knees and gave in to the memories of just seeing him again.

Tall, tanned, so strong when he'd caught her in his arms…

And how feeble had *that* been on her part!

She hugged her knees harder, protecting the secret in her heart—the knowledge of just how deep her love for him really was.

But love was generous, and kind, which meant that she had to leave him free to live the life he wanted, the life he'd planned and worked towards since he was ten.

Which meant the sooner she got out of the way the better.

Full of new resolve, she stood up and finished unpacking her purchases, crumpling up the note with the iron supplement on it—the note that had given away her secret.

She'd get onto the computer and look for jobs.

Would they need embryologists in Antarctica? Or Kazakhstan perhaps?

Impossible—she'd have the child.

And *that* refocused her thoughts, pleasing her so much she patted her as yet undistended belly and got down to sensible work.

Steve got through the weekend somehow, waking early on Monday morning and heading into his clinic to check all was well.

One of his colleagues met him when he was reading through the latest success rates—quite good as they were up about one per cent.

'I'd like some advice about a patient,' James told him. 'She's had two full cycles of IVF and two implants of embryos that had been frozen, all with no success. But this last cycle, the follicles failed to respond to stimuli and we were unable to get any eggs. Should we give her a longer break before the next cycle or is it likely that she just doesn't have any more eggs and will probably go into early menopause?'

It was as if a light bulb had suddenly lit up in Steve's brain, but right now he had to turn it off and work through the problem with his employee.

'Maybe discuss having a break—not long, perhaps a month to get her body back into normal cycles—then shall we see if we can get some immature eggs and use them for IVM?'

James grinned at him.

'Now, why didn't I think of that?'

'Because it's very new and we haven't done it here as yet, but on this last trip to Vanuatu we did successfully grow the eggs to maturity and ended up with two embryos, one implanted and one frozen for future use.'

'So, we'll do this? Do we need a specialist embryologist for the eggs? You'll help me with the retrieval?'

Steve smiled at his young colleague's excitement.

'Yes, and yes, and yes,' he said. 'I know just the

embryologist and am reasonably sure I can borrow her for a week or so while the eggs mature.'

'Great!'

James positively bounded out of the room, while Steve picked up the phone and called Andy.

'I know I'm begging again but the only IVM I've done so far was on Vanuatu, with Fran to nurture the immature eggs. I'd only need her for a few days—a week at most, not for a month.'

'I'm sure she'd be delighted,' Andy told him. 'We should all be trading staff when different skills are needed, it's how the younger ones can learn.'

Steve promised to let Andy know at least a week ahead and hung up the phone with a feeling of great satisfaction.

So, back to the light bulb…

He thought back to the island but couldn't remember just when the particular conversation had come up. What he *did* remember was Fran coming to ask him about the other couple—the one where the wife hadn't responded to the treatment and had no eggs ready for retrieval.

He'd been struck at the time by a shadow passing over Fran's face—a look of such sorrow he'd wanted to hug her, but there must have been others around, or maybe she'd left suddenly, not wanting him to see her sadness.

Had she suffered a similar problem on that third cycle of IVF, and had *her* gynaecologist suggested a lack of eggs and early menopause?

That would explain her determination to not marry him, her peculiar argument that he wanted children, plural, not just one child.

She'd be seeing this child as a miracle, conceived when one last egg had emerged and met his sperm.

And she'd *ached* for a child—she'd said that one day.

It wasn't that she didn't love him but because she *did* love him, and loving him wanted him to have his family.

Daft woman...

'You're lending me to him again!'

Fran couldn't recall ever having yelled at Andy,

but yell she did. Not that it did anything to flutter his normal calm complacency.

'It's only for a few days to help the eggs mature. He's not done IVM at his clinic in Alexandria, so hasn't anyone with experience in maturing the eggs. He said you did splendidly in Vanuatu, and you can show other lab workers exactly what you do.'

This completely rational statement left Fran speechless. She should have done more about finding another job, but for all she might wish she *was* in Timbuktu, deep inside she quivered at the thought of being so far away—in truth, so far from Steve.

Stupid, really.

What she had to worry about now was acting normally in his clinic, concentrating on the eggs and on showing his lab staff how she worked.

With him close by?

It would take some fortitude but she would do it and do it well. The couple whose eggs she was caring for deserved nothing but her best effort.

Which was all very well in theory but when

she walked into the clinic, looking around at this place Steve had set up, meeting nursing staff, admin people, partners, and finally lab staff, her knees were like jelly and her stomach bunched so tightly she hoped the tiny life inside her wasn't being affected by it.

He was there to greet her, of course, and it was he who introduced her around, his body so close it took all her strength not to lean in to it, or to brush her arm against his or let their fingers touch.

And he was there again at the end of the day, when the other lab staff had left and she was sitting at a bench, writing up a list of nutrients her little eggs would need.

'I love you, Fran,' he said, the words so unexpected she nearly fell off her stool.

He came closer, close enough to touch but not touching.

'And I think you love me.'

She looked at him then, looked into eyes that were echoing his words.

'And I think this stupid nonsense about not marrying me is all to do with children, right?'

She didn't answer, couldn't—couldn't deny, and couldn't confirm.

'Love is about making the loved one happy. It is generous—and giving—and that's you to a T. You're rejecting me because you think I need a woman who can give me children—as many children as I want—but how fair would it be to marry that woman when I couldn't offer her love?'

'Of course you could offer her love. What we had—it was madness—and its intensity led us—you—to believe it was love.'

He smiled.

'Gave yourself away there with the "us",' he teased, and she thought her heart would break.

'Okay, us,' she conceded. 'But does love like that last? And can't people, over a lifetime, love more than once? I loved Nigel, loved him deeply when we married. Yet now I haven't one iota of feeling for him.'

She paused, then added, 'Though in all honesty he went out of his way to kill that love so perhaps that doesn't count.'

Steve laughed, and shook his head.

'And that's just one of the things I love about you,' he said.

'What?' Fran demanded, unable to see anything funny in this conversation and still uncertain as to where it was leading.

'That you *are* honest. You might fumble about a bit from time to time, but usually the truth comes bursting out. You could have denied you were pregnant until you'd thought a bit more about it, but you couldn't. So...'

He stepped closer so he was right across the bench from her, then continued, 'Are you refusing to marry me because you think you can't produce the children I want? Or have you taken your wild imagination another step to where I might walk away from you because of that?'

Fran stared at him. He was right, she couldn't lie—not easily.

But to tell the truth?

He'd walked around the bench and stood close

enough for her to touch him, touch his hand, his face, but he touched her first, resting one hand against her cheek.

'Fran?' he prompted, and as emotion overwhelmed her she could only nod.

Then he was kissing her, telling her how stupid she had been, as if the love they shared could be dismissed, no matter how practical the reasons.

And her heart opened to his words so she could tell him of *her* love, although as they stopped for air she looked up into his face and asked, 'But the children?'

He smiled and kissed the tip of her nose.

'Let's just see what nature will provide and if this one turns out to be an only child then we do what Pop and Hallie did and take in kids in need of two very loving parents. Would that work for you?'

She shook her head, but this time in wonder, then nodded in answer to his question, which led to another kiss then a suggestion that they go home.

'My place is nearer,' Steve said.

CHAPTER TEN

ONCE SHE GOT over the astonishment that 'his place' was a mansion right on the shores of Sydney Harbour, and the initial doubts that she could live in a place like this, Fran gave in to the joy, and delight, and excitement, that came with being in love.

They walked hand in hand around the garden, looking out at the magnificent view, east towards the Heads and west towards the Opera House. Steve plucked one of the hibiscus flowers from bushes that ran rampant in the garden, and settled it securely behind her left ear, with a kiss and a murmured, 'Mine!'

'It's huge,' Fran said of the house, uncertain about his wealth now, uncertain she belonged.

'Don't give it a thought,' he assured her. 'I had an apartment in town for a long time, but after

Liane died, it had too many memories for me so I sold it. And, anyway, now the people I see as my family are growing up, it's good to have the space for them to come and stay. Liane's daughter Nikki will be down in the Christmas holidays—she's doing very junior work experience at the university, wants to be a scientist.'

'Not that you have to worry about the size of the house or visitors,' Steve hurried on to explain. 'I just use the bottom floor. It used to be servants' quarters but it's got the great views as well. And I've a live-in housekeeper, Molly, who takes care of the upstairs, visitors and all.'

Fran heard the words but could barely take them in, and looking at the house—mansion— she knew it should be filled with children and doubts assailed her once again.

'Stop it,' Steve said, picking up on her uncertainties. 'It's just a house and if you hate it, then we'll move.'

He took her in his arms and kissed her, long and hard, and, in kissing him back she released all the emotion that had been building since she'd left the island. So it wasn't surprising when he whispered, 'Maybe indoors?' and led her up onto a patio, and through French doors leading into an area that must have been either extensively renovated or had been very luxurious servants' quarters.

And again doubts assailed her.

'I don't think I'm up to this,' she whispered. 'I don't belong in a place like this.'

Steve eased her away from his body so he could see her face.

'You mean a home? That's all this is, Fran, my home. Our family's home! And if the family grows as we would like it to, then we'll banish the guests down here and we'll shift upstairs to fit them all in. Did I tell you Pop and Hallie's home was an old nunnery? It's how they managed to house so many waifs and strays. Can't we do that?'

She read the excitement in his eyes and realised it was echoed deep within her.

'Yes, I'd like that,' she said, already thinking of a young girl in her apartment block whose abusive stepfather was making her life miserable. Yes, there'd be laws to protect the children and hoops to be jumped through, and her own baby to consider, but, yes, the idea of being able to build a special family was truly wonderful.

They flew to Braxton the following Friday, to be met by a tall, charming, blond and blue-eyed man who greeted Steve with a bow.

'Sir Stephen,' he said, then enveloped Steve in a warm hug.

'And this is Francesca? My, Steve, she's a vast improvement on that woman you thought you were going to marry.'

He took Fran's hand and kissed her fingers.

'Welcome to the madness,' he said with a smile that could probably charm the kookaburras she could hear down from their trees.

'Just ignore him,' Steve was saying. 'If it wasn't for the fact that he can give us a lift home in his little helicopter, I wouldn't have told him we were coming.'

'Liar!' Marty responded. 'There's not one of us

that wouldn't turn up to meet the woman Steve's going to marry. Well, none of us that were all here at the same time. If everyone turned up we'd have to hire the village hall.'

Grabbing Fran's bag, he led the way back out of the building and across the tarmac to where a little helicopter stood.

'Mad about choppers,' Steve said to Fran. 'Women, too!' he added, and Marty laughed.

'He's actually a paramedic but now flies the rescue helicopter out of Braxton. It's doubly useful to have a pilot with advanced paramedic experience.' Steve paused, turning to Marty. 'Which reminds me, Marty, a woman I know, Emma Crawford, is coming up to work at Braxton A and E. You'll probably run into her some time.'

'You let him know other women?' Marty teased as they climbed into the little vehicle, Marty insisting Fran sit up front so she could see the view so Steve was crowded with the bags in the back.

'What's this Sir Stephen thing?' she asked Marty, who grinned in response while Steve gave her a stern order to just look at the view.

Which was spectacular! They rose first over a fairly large town, then thick rainforest, until the coast appeared, the dark blue ocean spreading out to the horizon, bordering headlands and curves of sandy bays.

'It's beautiful,' Fran said, and both the men agreed, something in their voices telling her it was also very special.

Then they were swooping low towards a small town set beside a golden arc of sand.

'Wetherby,' the two men chorused, and again their voices told her it was special.

She knew why Steve had been here, but Marty?

She could find out later, because now they had banked over a large, grim-looking building and were settling down onto a flat mown paddock behind it.

'The Nunnery!' Marty announced, waving his hand towards the building. 'And the garden between it and us is where we poor foster children slaved endlessly.'

'In between the beatings,' Steve put in, and both men laughed.

Clambering out wasn't quite as easy as getting in and by the time they were all out, with the luggage, a tall, plump woman was bustling towards them.

'Hallie!' Steve cried, lifting her in his arms and swinging her around.

'Put me down, I've told you not to do that!' she said, though obviously no one took any notice for now Marty was swinging her around too.

Back on her feet and looking only slightly flustered, she came towards Fran.

'My dear, I cannot tell you how happy I am that Stephen has finally met the woman of his dreams.'

And with that she enveloped Fran in a warm hug.

'Now, we'll ignore those two idiots, they'll have a lot to catch up on, just come inside and tell me all about yourself.'

She took Fran's arm and led her through the burgeoning garden to a much-used back door.

'We practically live in the kitchen,' she explained, 'although these days most of the time it's only me and Pop. Plenty of the children who lived here come back, but the time Marty and Steve were here was special as there were a number of them about the same age, so they really bonded. You'll meet Izzy later, she's coming to dinner with Nikki, who was Liane's daughter.'

The chatter stopped rather abruptly and Hallie studied Fran for a moment.

'Has Steve spoken to you of Liane?'

Fran nodded.

'He told me how troubled she was—broken, I think he said—and how he'd always loved her. Then how she'd got back on drugs and died after her daughter was born.'

'That daughter is our Nikki! Well, Izzy and Mac's Nikki really but…we like to think of her as a little bit ours.'

Hallie said the name as if, of all the children who'd passed through her hands, Nikki was special to her.

Fran thought back, then remembered Nikki had been a drug-addicted baby and all the care in rearing her that that would have entailed. Izzy would have needed help and no doubt that help would have come from Hallie.

No wonder Nikki was special!

'And your own family?' Hallie asked.

Fran smiled.

'Just a mother and she's climbing mountains in South America at the moment, although I did manage to catch her in a place where there was network coverage a few days ago and tell her about Steve.'

'Climbing mountains in South America?' Hallie echoed, and Fran's smile grew wider.

'That's how I felt when she first announced her plan. My father left us when I was young and Mum did all she could to make sure I got a good education. She worked two jobs and scrimped and saved so I could go to private school because I was interested in science and she felt I'd get better science teachers in a private school.'

She paused, thinking how much more she understood about her mother now—because she was pregnant?

She didn't know, but as she talked to Hallie

about the woman who had always preached restraint, who had written up weekly timetables
for study, meals and chores, and to whom good
manners were more important than a degree, she
began to understand her mother.

'I think she put so much into my life, to ensure
I had a good job, a safe marriage, a happy family, that she did nothing for herself.'

She paused, wondering how to put her mother
into words.

'She was devastated when my first marriage
broke down, but when I talked to her about it,
told her it was better to be without a man than
to be tied to someone who no longer loved me,
she not only understood but she saw *her* life in
a different light. She threw in her job and went
travelling, mostly in mountainous areas, insisting you see things more clearly in mountain air.'

Hallie laughed.

'I don't do mountains but I often climb up onto
the roof here—it's flat and quite safe—to think
about things.'

The men came in, obviously in search of the tea she and Hallie had failed to make.

'Not to worry,' Marty said. 'We boys will do it.' He turned to Fran.

'You'll find he's been totally domesticated so don't spoil it by waiting on him hand and foot.'

The man they all called Pop came in as they were demolishing a freshly baked sponge cake.

He greeted Fran warmly, then congratulated her.

'I've had some good lads come through here—even count that bloke Marty among them—but Steve's special so you be good to him.'

'Or you'll go down and bash her up?' Marty teased.

And although Pop smiled, he nodded towards Fran.

'I'm quite sure Fran knows what I mean.'

It was her turn to nod. It wasn't anything she could put into words but deep down she knew the words were true. Steve *was* special.

After a riotous dinner during which she'd some-how promised Nikki she could be a bridesmaid at her wedding, assured Izzy that of course she'd take care of Steve and had admitted, under Mac's acute questioning that, yes, she was pregnant, she and Steve were able to escape upstairs.

'Not to my old bedroom,' he explained to her as he led her along a corridor. 'This is a little flat that Pop made for Izzy when she and Nikki came home from Sydney. They use it for visitors now those two are living with Mac in the old doctor's house.'

He led her into the tiny living room, closed the door, and put his arms around her.

'Are you okay?' he asked, running his fingers through her hair and massaging her shoulders. 'It's been a big day and they're all mad, that lot.'

But Fran heard the love he felt for every one of them.

'Very okay,' she told him, nestling closer.

He showed her the main bedroom and bathroom, then helpfully stripped off her clothes, all the while telling her of his love, so in the end they left the shower until later, needing only to be together in the best possible way.

It wasn't until they were finally in bed that she was able to repeat the question she'd asked earlier.

'Why Sir Stephen?'

He laughed and pulled her close, so her head rested on his shoulder.

'I had the two grandparents as you know, one from each side of the family. I imagine, as they lived next door to each other and both of them had housekeepers and gardeners, gossip travelled fairly swiftly between the two houses. So, my grandmother would send me a cricket set at the beginning of summer, and within days my grandfather would send a better one. I think we eventually had enough sets to kit out an entire team.'

'Did they compete at birthdays and Christmas as well?' Fran asked, smiling at the thought of the orphan boy receiving all these gifts.

'Of course—stupendous gifts just kept arriving, so many I could share them around all the kids.'

'Ah,' Fran murmured, 'hence Sir Stephen—the noble knight dispensing gifts!'

Steve chuckled and held her closer, because for some reason, now he was back in the place that had become his true home, she felt more truly his.

'Want a run?' he asked when she opened bleary eyes next morning. 'Please,' he added, 'it's a special run.'

She was out of bed within minutes, showering and pulling on a T-shirt and shorts then light sneakers and joining him as he led the way out of the still sleeping house.

He pointed out the hospital on the way down towards the beach, and the old colonial house where Izzy and Mac lived with Nikki, then they were on the coastal path.

'We've all run it at different times—in fact, Izzy met Mac on it—but you must admit it's special.'

He looked at the woman he loved, wanting her to see the beauty of the place he loved.

'Very special,' she assured him, and it took all his strength of character not to kiss her there and then, because he knew he'd probably have followed the kiss by dragging her into the sand dunes.

So they ran, slowly, to take in the beauty of the craggy headlands and the curving bays, the wind-bent casuarinas and crashing waves that broke against the cliffs.

They stopped at a fresh water tap, there to serve people walking the coastal path, which stretched for miles along this part of the coast.

They drank freely then stood up, looking out at the little curve of golden sand, the surf rolling in gently, the smell of the ocean drawn deep into their lungs.

Side by side in this beautiful place, arms around each other's waists, Steve could only think that this must be perfection.

'I love you, Francesca Hawthorne,' Steve said, taking her hand and lifting it to his lips to drop a kiss into her palm then close her fingers around it.

'And I you,' she said, then gave him a kiss to hold in *his* palm.

Which, Steve decided as they came back into Wetherby, must have made them both look quite demented, striding along, each with one hand closed firmly on a kiss...

EPILOGUE

IT WAS LATE summer when the family gathered
for the wedding, a bright, cool day with a light
breeze whipping up a few cheeky wavelets on
the harbour.

Fran's mother had arrived two days earlier, and
it seemed to Fran they'd hardly stopped talking
since she'd landed at the airport. They'd talked
of her mother's marriage and Fran's childhood,
remembering, laughing and sometimes crying.

With her mother's help, Fran slid into the light
summer dress she'd chosen for her wedding.
Cream, with a scattering of bright red flowers,
not hibiscus but close enough to have reminded
her of the island.

'Do you like it?' she asked, arms held out as
she twirled in front of her mother, the soft silk

of the material swirling from a band beneath her bust.

'Love it,' her mother said. 'And so will Steve when he sees that neckline!'

Immediately wary, Fran lifted her hands to cover the hint of depth between her breasts, and her mother laughed.

'It's wonderful,' she assured Fran. 'I was only teasing you. Now, you're sure about this?'

Fran looked into her mother's eyes.

'More sure than I've ever been of anything in my life. I love him, Mum, more than I had ever imagined loving anyone.'

'And Nigel?'

Fran grinned. 'Who's Nigel?'

And they both laughed, but the conversation brought them to the subject of love.

'We've both loved badly,' her mother said softly, 'but seeing you with Steve I know how right this marriage is. Don't ever be afraid to give freely of your love. I didn't know that when I married. I was brought up to not show emotion and I probably taught you that as well, but love is so precious you have to nurture it so it flourishes in every corner of your life for ever.'

A light tap at the door, and as her mother hurried to open it, Fran looked out over the harbour, sparkling in the sunshine, the ferries like toy boats a child might play with in the bath.

She patted her stomach then rested her hand on the bulge, thinking of this child in the bath with boats.

Or on a boat going over to the Zoo, perhaps growing up to be a doctor...

Or not, it didn't matter, for not only was this the child she'd never thought to have, but it was Steve's child and doubly precious for that!

Nikki arrived, looking stunning in red, her dress the same design as Fran's and, in Nikki's opinion, *very* grown-up!

'Oh, you look fabulous!' she said, and the expression on her face told Fran she meant it.

'And so do you,' Fran told her, 'but what's the box?'

'Oh, I forgot! Steve said to give it to you.'

She handed Fran a clear plastic box. Nestled inside it was a brilliant red hibiscus.

Opening the box, Fran saw the note.

'Which ear?' Steve had written, and Fran laughed. She lifted the flower, and going to the mirror settled it behind her left ear.

'Definitely taken,' she said, smiling at her mother and Nikki, who both shook their heads at the strange wedding headdress.

'It's time,' her mother said. 'You really want to do this?'

Fran could only smile, but she kissed her mother and gave her a tight hug, blinking back tears as her mother took her hand to lead her and Nikki down the stairs and out through the garden to a gazebo at the edge of the property, where, with friends and family around them, and the harbour sparkling behind them, they promised to love and honour each other for the rest of their lives.

The guests drifted back to the terrace where drinks and food was being served,

But Steve held Fran's hand and looked out over the beautiful view.

'I love you, Francesca Louise Ransome,' he said softly, 'with all my heart and mind and body.'

Then he drew her close—or as close as her belly allowed—and kissed her, ignoring the wolf whistles from his family on the terrace behind them.

* * * * *

*If you enjoyed this story, check out
these other great reads from
Meredith Webber:*

*ENGAGED TO THE DOCTOR SHEIKH
A FOREVER FAMILY FOR THE ARMY DOC
A SHEIKH TO CAPTURE HER HEART
THE MAN SHE COULD NEVER FORGET*

All available now!

SAME GREAT STORIES...
STYLISH NEW LOOK!

We're having a makeover!
From next month we'll still be bringing
you the very best romance from authors
you love, with a fabulous new look.

LOOK OUT FOR OUR STYLISH NEW LOGO, TOO

MILLS & BOON

LET'S TALK

Romance

For exclusive extracts, competitions
and special offers, find us online:

f facebook.com/millsandboon

⌾ @millsandboonuk

🐦 @millsandboon

Or get in touch on 0844 844 1351*

For all the latest titles coming soon,
visit millsandboon.co.uk/nextmonth